Lumberjack Werebear

(Saw Bears, Book 1)

T. S. JOYCE

Lumberjack Werebear

ISBN-13: 978-1537783550
ISBN-10: 1537783556
Copyright © 2015, T. S. Joyce
First electronic publication: February 2015

T. S. Joyce
www.tsjoyce.com

NOTE FROM THE AUTHOR:
This book is a work of fiction. The names, characters, places, and incidents are products of the writer's imagination or have been used fictitiously and are not to be construed as real. Any resemblance to persons, living or dead, actual events, locale or organizations is entirely coincidental. The author does not have any control over and does not assume any responsibility for third-party websites or their content.

Published in the United States of America

First digital publication: February 2015
First print publication: September 2016

Editing: Corinne DeMaagd

ONE

The brakes on Brooke Belle's Volvo screeched as she pulled to a stop and glared at the sign above her front window.

Asheland Mobile Park, it read.

Mobile park? Her mentor, Meredith, had described the rustic oasis she was going to be spending the next three weeks in as if it was a row of quaint Victorian cottages nestled near Saratoga, Wyoming. Not a trailer park.

She shook her phone, as if the GPS was to blame, and rechecked the address Meredith had scribbled onto a notecard. She should've known something was amiss when she had to travel an hour outside of town to end up here.

The sun was sinking behind scenic mountains that stood guard over the ten tiny mobile homes in front of her. No way did she want to brave those switchbacks again in the dark. She'd barely survived the winding roads to get here in broad daylight. With a muttered curse, she eased forward and parked in front of the first trailer on the left that had an *Office* sign over the front door.

Her brakes squeaked again, but she wasn't embarrassed. The concrete pad she parked on was cracked like a spider web and was sprouting an interestingly-shaped weed garden. No one was going to judge her here.

Slowly, cautiously, she stepped from the safety of her car and made her way up the creaking porch stairs to the office. After opening the screen door, she knocked soundly on the inner one, which seemed to be made of plywood held together by mold. Wiping her knuckles on her jeans, she waited. And waited.

Where was everyone?

She narrowed her eyes at the shadows that stretched across the dirt road and bisected two rows of trailers. She blew air out of her cheeks with impatience. A few old pickup trucks sat in front of some of the houses, but from the way the grass was hugging the tires, they'd likely been there for a while.

Well, shitsicles. No one was here. Now what was she supposed to do?

"Are you lost?" a deep voice sounded from beside the porch.

Brooke started and jumped back. "Balls!" She clasped her chest like it would keep her skittering heart inside. "You scared me."

A tall, stocky man leaned against the corner of the office with his arms crossed as if he'd been there the entire time. The frown on his face made it hard to tell if he was handsome or not. "I asked if you were lost."

"Hopefully." She cleared her throat and straightened her spine. "Could you help me figure out if I've made a wrong turn somewhere? I'm looking for 1010 Asheford Drive. I'm supposed to be renting a cabin for a few weeks."

The man's eyebrows shot up, exposing his dark eyes beneath. His gaze drifted to a dilapidated trailer, and a chuckle rumbled from his chest. "Miss, if you're looking for a vacation home of some sort, you rented the wrong one."

Brooke pursed her lips and absorbed the appearance of the small trailer smack dab in the middle of the park. From here, it clearly read 1010, if she ignored that the last zero was dangling and hanging on by one last rusty nail.

She was going to kill Meredith.

"Name's Bruiser," the man said with a grin.

"Bruiser?"

"Uh huh."

"Your parents thought about it, and the name they came up with for their child was Bruiser?"

"Aren't you a judgy little thing? Since you're so curious about my upbringing, no. They named me Horace, which got me taunted as a kid until I grew big enough to beat the shit out of my bullies. They were the ones who gave me the name Bruiser."

"I didn't mean to…" She inhaled deeply and started again. "I'm sorry. It's been a long day, and this place," she said, holding her hands up helplessly, "wasn't what I expected it to be."

"I'd imagine not. Wait here, and I'll get someone who can help you." The corner of his lip twitched as he turned and strode to the trailer next door. "Connor," he called, banging on the metal side of the house. "Need your help with something."

"What the fuck, Bruiser?" a man called from inside. He ducked under the too short door, buckling his belt with a look of pure fury on his face. "Today is one of my days off. All I ask is for one day where I don't have to wear any gosh danged…" His eyes drifted to her, and he froze. "Pants," he finished. He was all ruffled blond hair and bewildered green eyes.

Brooke snorted. Really, she tried to hide the laugh, but she hadn't known there was such a thing as a pants-off day.

"It's not funny," he muttered, gripping the railing of his porch. "What do you want?"

"Uhh, a friend of mine rented a house for me. *Bruiser* over here tells me I have the right address, and that you can help me."

Connor's eyes went wide. "Brooke Belle?"

Her heart sank to the toes of her sneakers. "That would be me."

"Holy shit, you showed up. And early. You weren't supposed to be here until next week. Hypothetically. If you showed up." He frowned.

"Which I never thought you would actually do, because look around. This ain't ideal for a vacation."

"That's what I said, and what are you talking about?" Bruiser asked, crossing his arms over his chest again until his biceps flexed. "No women up here. You know the rules. We aren't into renting to strangers, either. Especially not high fallutin' city slickin' judgy judgertons like this one. No offense," he said as he flicked his attention to her, then away.

"None taken." She didn't want to hunker down in hillbilly town any more than Bruiser wanted her here.

Connor took his time looking her up and down. Suddenly feeling vulnerable, she swallowed hard and clasped her hands in front of her thighs.

"Meredith sent her," was all Connor said before he stepped lightly down his porch stairs and sauntered over to the office where she stood.

She could've sworn he sniffed her hair as he passed to pull the front door open. Creepy.

Bruiser chuckled. His chuckling then turned to laughter as he bent at the waist and locked his hands on his knees, chortling until he wheezed. The ass. "Ho!" he said, standing and wiping moisture from the corners of his eyes. "Tagan is going to lose it when he finds out about her." Bruiser pointed to Connor and grinned. "He's gonna bleed you."

"Shut up," Connor muttered, then disappeared inside.

Talk of bleeding people jacked up Brooke's discomfort another notch. She took a seat in front of the desk in a cracked faux leather chair that Connor had pointed to.

He sank into a matching seat behind the desk. "You got a boyfriend back home?"

"What?"

"A boyfriend, a lover, bedmate, whatever. You got a man waiting for you?"

"That's none of your business."

Connor was trouble. If she hadn't suspected his unwanted intentions before, this question would've sealed it. She definitely wasn't looking for any male attention. "I should go." She should've left the second she saw the sign for the mobile park. Now, she'd lost precious minutes of daylight.

"Pipe down. I'm not asking for me. Well," he said with a wink. "Not only for me."

"Bruiser's not my type," Brooke gritted out.

"Fair enough," he murmured as he rifled through a desk drawer. "Here." He tossed her a key, which she wasn't ready for and dropped on the floor. "Nice reflexes."

To hide her irritation from the idiot behind the desk, she leaned over to retrieve the key, giving the carpet a dirty look. "Thanks, but no thanks. I really should be going. Meredith made some sort of mistake. I don't belong here."

"Damned straight you don't, but unless you want to navigate back roads in the dark, I'd suggest you make yourself cozy in trailer 1010."

Okay, the mention of those roads in the dark did scare her enough to clutch the key. "Does it lock?" A.K.A—could she escape the hair-sniffer who was looking at her boobs right now?

"'Course it does. That one's got a fancy double lock and everything."

She shouldn't stay. Her danger radar was blaring off the hook, but her options were limited. Stay here until the crack of dawn when she could barrel out of this dump or get lost in the dark. In the woods. Without food or water.

"Thank you," she said through clenched teeth.

Connor leaned back with an arrogant smile and hooked his hands behind his head. "You're welcome, princess."

"It's just Brooke."

"All right then, you have a nice day...princess."

Swallowing the verbal lashing that was clawing its way up her throat, she stood, smoothed the wrinkles from her jeans, then marched out the front door.

One night here, and then she was gone. She'd rent a room in Saratoga and try to heal her broken muse there. Anything would be better than with a couple of burly, foul-mouthed, irritating men.

One night, then Asheland Mobile Park would be nothing but a blotch in her rearview mirror.

TWO

Trailer 1010 was in better shape on the inside than it looked like on the outside. It was old, and there was a giant dead spider on the counter, but someone had taken the time to put dark wood laminate flooring in and had recently painted the walls and cabinets. The chemical smell still clung to the air. A green couch sat in front of a small entertainment center, and the kitchen wasn't disgusting, so there was that. It was actually cuter than she imagined a house like this could be. White cabinets, a deep sink, a purring refrigerator, and wainscoting around the tiny breakfast nook walls, and this place was downright passable as a viable living space. It even had a surprising amount of character.

She kicked a small pile of leftover lumber out of the doorway of the bedroom attached to the kitchen and nodded her head slowly at the decent size of the bedroom. A small bathroom was just on the other side. Brown-colored shower, outdated light fixtures, and a horrid looking faux marble sink with burn marks said the bathroom hadn't been updated like the rest of the house, but when she turned on the faucet, it worked, so it would be good enough for the night. She'd never seen a washer and dryer in a bathroom before, but she supposed trailer designers had to get creative with space in a tiny home like this.

Back across the living room, a large second bedroom and bathroom took up nearly half the trailer. If she were staying, which she wasn't, this was where she would've set up her temporary art studio.

"First thing's first," she muttered, checking the window lock.

The pane was old, and the seal had broken sometime in the trailer's long history since a cool breeze brushed her skin and raised chill bumps on her arms. She made sure it was nice and secure. The rest of the windows were the same, all drafty. She rubbed her arms to bring some warmth back into them and began to unfold the clean-smelling sheets and comforter someone had thoughtfully placed on the end of the queen-size mattress. At least the bed had a frame and stood off the ground, in case any of those terrifying spiders were still lurking about.

"They're back," Connor called out, scaring the devil out of Brooke.

She looked around frantically. She could've sworn she locked the door behind her, but he sounded as if he were right beside her. Heart pounding, she moved the thin blue curtain to the side and watched Connor give a two fingered wave to someone she couldn't see. Her mouth hung open. The walls must be thin as paper for her to hear him so easily. She eyeballed the width of the wall connected to the window, and it was less than three inches thick. Huh. She narrowed her eyes at the sagging ceiling and hooked her hands on her hips. Hopefully, the place would stand for one more night until she was out of here.

Movement caught her eye, and her attention jerked to a small brown mound that skittered across the floor and into the bathroom. A mouse!

A scream, the pitch of which she'd never heard come from her vocal chords, shrieked from her. Instinctively, she bolted away from the critter, hands in the air as her legs pumped through the kitchen and living room. Chills ran up her spine as she imagined it chasing her. Gasping to scream again, she fumbled with the front door lock. A whimper turned into a high-pitched squawk just as she threw open the door.

A man holding a yellow hard hat ran into her full-force, and they fell back into the entryway.

When she screamed again, the man closed his blazing blue eyes and hunched into himself as if the sound physically hurt him.

"Woman, stop it! What's wrong?" The man looked around frantically, as if he was searching for the danger.

Brooke felt something touch her hair. "It's in my hair! It's in my hair, isn't it?"

"What?" He searched her hair from his position right on top of her.

"The mouse!"

He froze, then his body relaxed. One dark eyebrow cocked up as he propped himself up on his elbows. "A mouse? Seriously? I thought you were dying."

He hovered over her, hips cradled between her legs, breathing hard like he'd just sprinted to her aid. His impossibly blue eyes searched her face, and something happened. Something instinctual. Something indiscernible sparked in the space between them. Mouse forgotten and chest heaving, she raked her gaze over his locked arms and bulging triceps. His hole-riddled gray T-shirt and the thick cords of muscle that peeked from it. His Adam's Apple bobbed as he swallowed hard, as if he were feeling the same stunned flare she was. Straight nose, dark skin covered in dirt and dried sweat, animated eyebrows, and dark hair cropped short. He was beautiful. Masculine as hell, but beautiful was the word that came to mind.

A crowd had apparently gathered outside because Bruiser's voice filled the entire house. "Looks like she's claimed boys. Tagan's already having his way with her."

The Tagan he spoke of looked down at their

connected hips with wide eyes, and scrambled off her like she'd just set his dick on fire.

He stood and slammed the door closed, cutting off the gawking view of what looked like six or seven men. Glowering, he stood over her and refused to offer her a hand when she stumbled getting up.

"Who the hell are you?" he asked, his voice low and gravelly. Sexy.

"Brooke Belle." Her name came out a squeak, which reminded her of the mouse. Jumping around him, she grabbed onto the back of his shirt with one hand and pointed to the bedroom with the other. "There's a giant mouse in there. Or a rat. Or a ferret or prairie dog, I don't know. It's huge." Damn her voice as it shook.

"I don't give a shit about some mouse, woman. What're you doing in my bunkhouse?"

"Your bunkhouse? No, no, no. There's been some mistake. I rented this place. Or rather, my mentor rented it."

Connor shoved his head through the door, face red like he was pissed. "I saw her first."

"Get out!" Tagan bellowed. He was terrifying.

Brooke covered her ears and cowered.

Connor narrowed his eyes and slowly shut the door.

"Fantastic," Tagan growled out, swinging his gaze to her. He jammed an accusing finger at the door. "And you caught the attention of that one? I want answers and now. Who. The hell. Are you?"

Brooke straightened her back and tipped her chin up primly. "I'll talk when you take care of the mouse."

"Take care of the—" With a snarl, he chucked his hard hat at the couch and stomped into the bedroom, leaving a mud trail behind him, the brute.

She was a little surprised he didn't go through the squishy parts in the floor with his clunking work boots. Not five seconds later, he came out holding the tail of the rodent—a small brown mouse and definitely not the size of a prairie dog. He swung it toward her until she backed into the wall, then disappeared outside with it. Another five seconds, and he was back inside, arms crossed, head cocked, eyes blazing, and apparently waiting for her to speak.

"I'm Brooke Belle, like I said, and I was under the assumption that my mentor had rented a cottage retreat for me. And then I came here, and it was not as expected."

"You can't stay here."

"Yeah, I get that, but I'm not comfortable finding Saratoga in the dark either. Connor told me I could stay the night and leave in the morning."

Tagan dragged a troubled gaze toward the door. "What else did Connor say to you?"

"That's none of your business."

"Yeah, it is! Connor is—" He ran his hands roughly through his short hair. "One night." He turned and opened the door, then said over his shoulder, "And I don't want you talking to Connor anymore. Is that clear?"

"Crystal."

"Great." He slammed the door so hard, it rattled the trailer.

****

Tagan gritted his teeth so hard, his jaw hurt. The woman had nearly drawn his bear from him, and for what? He didn't know her. Why the hell was his animal so desperate to rip out of his skin around a complete stranger? His hands shook, so he gripped his waist and gave a withering look to his crew. The entirety of the Ashe Crew, minus Jed, his alpha, was standing below the porch with somber expressions.

"Is she staying?" Kellen asked. The man was almost as tall as Tagan, but where Tagan's eyes were bright blue, Kellen's were the rich color of coffee. The scar across his jaw said he fought like a warrior, but still, Kellen couldn't hold his gaze. Not when Tagan's bear was riled up like this.

"Of course she isn't staying. She's not a plaything. She's..." Human. She was a fucking human in a clan of monsters.

"We could take care of her," Kellen said low.

Tagan drew up, shocked to his core. "Take care of her? She isn't Snow White, and we aren't the seven dwarves. She doesn't belong here. No woman does."

He sighed and looked at the flimsy front door of her trailer. She no doubt had terrible hearing like the rest of her kind, but the walls were thin, and she could probably make out every word he was saying.

"Look, she's leaving first thing in the morning. I don't want any of you bothering her, okay?" He glared at Connor to make sure he agreed to his order. Tagan was second in the clan, and when Jed was away, his word was law.

Connor nodded once and stared at the ground.

Still, he trusted Connor about as far as he could throw him. Or rather, he didn't trust his bear. His inner animal had been on a relentless hunt for a mate lately, and Tagan would be damned if Connor was going to attach to some human who posed a threat to all of them. If he wanted a mate so badly, he needed to take a leave of absence from the crew and track down a she-bear who was willing. One who could better handle Connor's violent appetites in the bedroom. One who was stronger than some human woman afraid of a harmless mouse.

A trill of dread snaked up Tagan's spine as Connor's attention shifted toward the trailer door again. The others dispersed, but Connor just stood there, as if he couldn't help himself, and his eyes lightened more with each passing second.

"Go on," Tagan said.

Connor drew his inhuman gaze to Tagan, then slowly slipped away.

Tagan sighed and pinched the bridge of his nose to ward away the oncoming headache that rested just behind his eyes.

That woman was in more trouble than she even knew.

A mouse in her trailer was the very least of her worries until she hightailed it out of here tomorrow morning.

THREE

Zero freaking bars, and Brooke was stifling the urge to chuck her cell phone at the wall. Every text she'd sent to Meredith had failed, and now she couldn't make a call out. Her GPS still seemed to work, so what gave?

With a growl, she snatched an oversized hoodie from her open suitcase on the bed and pulled it on. Before she could change her mind, she threw open the door and shoved the phone as far into the air as her arm would stretch. The smell of steak hit her nostrils and elicited an immediate rumble from her stomach. She hadn't eaten since lunch, and down the road, the Asheford Drive hermits seemed to be having a jovial bonfire.

Still no bars.

Huffing a sigh, she cast a baleful glare at the mountain men laughing and talking by the fire, shoved her phone in her hoodie pocket, and bounded down the stairs. She was on the side of a mountain, and surely, if she got high enough, she could get a signal.

She clicked on the pen light that hung from her keychain and made her way behind the trailer to a rickety gate that screeched when she opened it.

"What're you doing?" Tagan asked.

She gasped. He stood leaning against the fence like he'd waited for days for her to try to make an escape.

"Not that it's any of your business, but I'm going to search for a signal for my cell phone. I need to make a call."

"To whom?"

"My mentor," she said. "She made a mistake sending me here, and I need her help to figure out where else I can stay for the rest of my trip.

Apparently, you don't get internet out here in the boonies either."

"You're hungry." It wasn't a question, but a statement.

Derailed from her irritation with Meredith, she asked, "What?"

"I can hear your stomach growling from here. Eat first, and then I'll show you the best place to get reception."

"I'm not following you out into the woods."

"Why not?"

"Because I don't trust you. I'm not stupid, Tagan. I've watched Deliverance."

A surprised-sounding laugh huffed from his chest, and his face cracked into a grin. In the flickering glow of the fire, one side of his face was washed in orange light that contrasted with the white of his teeth. "You must think mighty low of me, Ms. Belle, but I assure you, I'm no danger to you."

"You yelled at me earlier." She didn't mean to sound like she was pouting. It just came out that way. She was an artist, a sensitive soul, and he'd been a brute during their first meeting.

The smile faded from his face, and he leaned his

lower back against the fence. He stared at the fire and the men talking around it. "If I hurt your feelings, I'm sorry. I'm not used to talking to...women."

Brooke snorted. "Obviously."

He canted his head and studied her face. "Why are you really here?"

She offered him a sad smile. "Because I lost my way."

"You mean you got lost on the way up here?"

"No. I mean, I needed a break from my life. I was afraid I'd never be able to find the good parts of myself again if I didn't take a break from everything I knew."

He stared at her for a long time, as if he was waiting for her to tell him her life story. No one had heard that tale, though, not even Meredith.

"What happened here?" He brushed her long, blond hair to the side and ran his finger along the bandage on her neck. He didn't quite touch her skin, but a shiver quaked up her spine and landed in her shoulders.

Tagan frowned and pulled his hand away.

"That is part of the reason I lost my way." The words were forced and thick in her throat. She tried to swallow down the traitorous tears that would tell him how broken she really was. "Now, if you'll excuse me, I think I can wait until tomorrow to call Meredith—"

"Meredith?" Tagan stood ramrod straight and squared his shoulders to hers.

She backed up a step as his eyes seemed to turn darker, a trick of the firelight, no doubt, but still terrifying. "My mentor. She was the one who rented your bunkhouse to me."

He shook his head, as if he didn't give two figs who her mentor was. "What do you do?"

"Pardon me?"

"For a living? What do you do for money?"

Her mouth dropped open at his audacity. "I'm a painter."

The smile he gave her failed to reach his eyes, and he nodded his head slowly. "Of course you are." He scrubbed his hands over his face and sauntered off.

"Wha— You are the rudest man I've ever met in my life." She followed, punching her sneakers into the earth. "So let me get this straight. I'm not allowed to have first impressions about this place, but you can judge me on my occupation? Which is actually a very lucrative career, I'll have you know." She yanked his arm and spun him. "I was good once!"

The last word echoed against the mountains, and the men at the fire grew quiet.

The harsh look in Tagan's eyes softened. His slow grip on her shoulders halted her trembling. When had she started shaking?

"Whatever happened to you, your mentor was wrong. It can't be fixed here. *You* can't be fixed here."

"I know." Her words came out ragged and defeated. Shame heated her cheeks, and she glanced at the men by the fire, all staring at her.

A tall man with dark hair styled longer on top scooted down a log and patted it. "You, girl. You'll sit here and eat with us. We'll feed you."

The way he spoke was odd, but the kind look in his deep brown eyes had her slipping from Tagan's grasp and settling in beside the man. "Thank you."

"I'm Kellen." He pointed to Connor and Bruiser and said, "You know them. That's Haydan."

A man with a shaved head and tattoo on his neck grunted and nodded, and Kellen went to the next around the fire.

"That's Drew."

Drew couldn't seem to meet her eyes, but he attempted to smile before he took another bite of beans.

"Those two over there, Brighton and Denison," Kellen said, "were born of the same sow."

"What does that mean?" she asked.

"He's my brother," Denison explained. He looked around the fire and gave a private smile at his plate. "I mean, he's my blood brother. Two minutes older than me. He don't talk, though. Never has."

Brighton studied her frankly, then nodded and grinned.

"Is this everyone who lives in this trailer park?" she asked, curiosity lining up a string of questions in her mind.

"All but one," Connor said. "Jedidiah is up in Saratoga, fucking his mate."

The men went silent and still, and a soft rumble came from one of them. It was an eerie sound that lifted the hairs on the back of her neck.

"What do you mean by mate?" Brooke asked softly, suddenly feeling exposed among these strangers.

"He doesn't mean anything," Tagan said in a steely voice. He handed her a plate he'd apparently made during introductions and sat on the other side of her, so close she could feel his warmth through the thick material of her hoodie.

The plate in her hands was metal and growing hot under the piping steak, baked potato, and beans. Gently, she set it on her lap and made sure everyone else was eating before she dug in.

"What do you paint?" Kellen asked between bites.

Brooke twisted on her rough seat and tried to judge the distance from where she and Tagan had been talking about her occupation. It should've been too far for him to hear, but apparently he had supersonic dog hearing or something.

"I paint mostly fantasy landscapes. The ones that were best received were in a series called The Stars Align."

"And what did they look like?"

"Uhh, they were set at night, but the forest below the starry sky was done in bright colors. Like the Northern Lights. I paint with extra on my brush and build up the canvas until the surface has texture.

Here." She pulled her phone from her pocket. The signal was still gone, but she could pull up pictures. She scrolled through a few she'd taken of the woods on the way up here for inspiration and handed the phone to Kellen.

Tagan was trying not to look as Kellen showed it around, she could tell, but his eyes landed on the phone the second Kellen angled it in his direction.

"I can draw horses," Haydan said. "If you ever need to paint one, I can start it for you."

Her face cracked in a smile, and she dipped her chin. The stretch of her face felt good.

"You have dimples," Tagan said, so low she almost missed his words.

Self-conscious, she nodded and sawed another piece off her steak. The food tasted amazing. Maybe it was because she was starving, but she was impressed with how good a group of bachelors could cook. "What do you all do?"

"For work?" Denison asked.

"Yeah."

Drew thumped his chest. "We're lumberjacks. Men of the ax. Wood cutters. The Paul Bunyons of the—"

"She gets it, Drew," Denison said, tossing a bean at him.

Brooke giggled at their easy rapport. "I've never met lumberjacks before. Honestly, I didn't realize they existed anymore around here."

The hint of a smile clung to the corners of Tagan's mouth as he said, "There weren't until a few months ago. The sawmill in Saratoga has been shut down for a decade, but the beetle infestation has them up and running again."

The mention of beetles made her want to lift her shoes off the ground. "Are there a lot of beetles still around here?"

"Hell, yeah. They're nearly impossible to kill off," Haydan said. "I can draw beetles, too."

"Shut up, man," Drew said, shoving his shoulder.

"The beetles have killed off a lot of this forest and left hundreds of thousands of dead trees," Tagan said. "They've dried and created the perfect tinder for wild fires. The mill in Saratoga is equipped to treat the beetle eaten wood, but they needed a few crews to come in and help clear the land. New growth has been slow. Because the woods were so thick, sunlight couldn't get to the pinecones beneath the thick branches. Once we come through and take out the dead trees, the forest will come back. Plus, we're re-planting as we go along. Takes a lot of time, but it'll be worth it to see this place green again."

"So, you aren't the only crew on this mountain?"

"On this mountain, yes," Kellen said. "We are the Ashe crew. The Gray Backs are over a ridge but still close enough to be a pain in our asses. The Boarlanders do the cutting for both crews. The man who hired us owns this land. Hundreds of thousands of acres need to be cleared, and each log is money in our pockets. The more timber we clear, the closer the crews get to each other."

"So, you have lumberjack battles?" She held back a laugh, imagining plaid-shirted, burly men yelling about territory disputes.

"Princess, you wouldn't want to be within a mile of one when it goes down," Connor said ominously.

She hated the way he called her that. She narrowed her eyes at him, then bent to the task of eating the rest of her meal before it cooled.

The rumbling noise sounded again, and when she looked up at Tagan, he was glaring at Connor. Stifling a gasp, she reached out before she could change her mind and pressed the palm of her hand against his rattling chest.

A second of deep vibration shook her hand before he grabbed her palm. The noise stopped, and Tagan looked at her with wide eyes. Confusion swam in the depths there, and he dropped his gaze to her palm. For an instant, she thought he would kiss it.

"What are you doing to me?" he asked, his tone soft but accusing.

"I said I saw her first," Connor gritted out, dropping his plate beside his feet and standing. "I won't fuckin' say it again."

Tagan stood so fast, he blurred.

"All right, dinner's through," Kellen said, dragging her backward off the log. When had the behemoth even stood up?

"I challenge you for her," Connor snarled, circling the fire. "And I challenge you for Second."

"Shit," Kellen muttered, hustling her away faster.

"Wait, what are they doing?" She tried to escape his grasp, but damn, Kellen was surprisingly strong.

"Nothing you need to worry about, and nothing that's gonna happen tonight, anyway. Challenges can't be done without Jed here."

He could've been talking in French. She didn't understand any of this. "Wait! My plate. I forgot to leave my plate."

"I'll take it back." Kellen had already managed to drag her past three trailers, and she was having trouble seeing Tagan and Connor in the middle of the men who seemed to be trying to pull them apart.

She didn't belong to anyone, and some archaic fight sure as sugar wasn't going to ensure that she picked either one of them. "I don't understand."

Kellen spun her shoulders and leveled her a look. "I want you to stay. I like you, and we never have soft things around here. I want us to take care of you and fix your paintings, but you don't want Connor. You don't. And Tagan isn't ready for a mate. Best you leave at first light in the morning."

"Okay," she said, her voice wrenching up an octave. Kellen was telling her something important. The desperate look in his eyes said so, but his words were jumbled. *Mate?* "I'll leave." She'd been planning on it, anyway.

Kellen's oversized hands slipped from her shoulders, and he looked back at her once as he walked back toward the men by the fire.

Whatever relaxed moment she'd found by the fire with those strangers, there was something much deeper going on here. Something she couldn't fathom, nor would she ever. These men were different from anyone she'd ever met. It took a certain kind of person to live out in the middle of nowhere, away from civilization, and it had apparently taken its toll on all of them.

Kellen, Tagan, and her own instincts had all warned her off Connor, and now he was going to try and hurt Tagan for some notion of dibs on her. Brooke's stomach lurched, and for a second, she thought she'd be sick right at the corner of 1010.

She was nobody's dibs, and Kellen didn't need to worry. As soon as dawn streaked the sky, she'd been speeding off in her Volvo.

Nothing, and no one, could make her stay.

FOUR

Heart pounding, trying to get away. A scream trapped in her throat. Brooke slammed against the wall as the stranger's palm connected with her cheek again. Whimpering. Was that from her? Scared, scared, scared.

"You stupid bitch. All you had to do was give me your purse." Fetid breath. Soulless voice.

Couldn't move. Crying. Tears burning tracks down her face. She was going to die in this stairwell. "I tried…" she whispered, desperate to explain. Purse wound around her arm. Couldn't hand it over fast enough. Now she'd die for clumsiness. "Please don't kill me."

Laughter, empty and cruel. Echoing down the empty stairs. Rotted teeth showed in an empty smile. A slash of light reflecting off silver. The blade.

"Not gonna kill you, darlin'. Gonna mark you so you always remember the day you fucked with me."

Pain, pain, pain.

"Nooo!" Brooke shot up in bed and fell over the edge. She couldn't breathe, and the mark on her neck burned like hellfire. Where was she? It was dark. Too dark.

Blue eyes, reflecting like an animal's in the dim light of the moon. Terror seized her throat, making it impossible to scream.

"Shhh," Tagan said, falling to his knees beside her.

"Don't touch me!" she sobbed, trying to fling his grip off her upper arms.

He didn't let go. Instead, he drew her into his lap and held her tight.

"Don't touch me," she said again with less feeling.

"It's okay. I'm here. No one is going to hurt you."

A low wail left her lips as she clutched onto his

T-shirt in the dark. Her tears were dampening the fabric, but she didn't care. For the first time since she'd been attacked, the touch of a man didn't frighten her. She didn't even flinch when he lifted his hand to stroke her hair away from her face.

She squeezed her eyes tightly closed and allowed him to rock her gently until her heart felt like it was back in her chest. He smelled like soap and piney woods with an undercurrent of something rich and masculine. She didn't deserve his comfort. She didn't deserve anyone's comfort.

Stupid fucking nightmare.

Every time it was the same.

Every time she had to relive the night that stripped everything from her.

When she opened her eyes again, they had adjusted to the minimal blue moonlight filtering in through the bedroom windows. Kellen crouched near her ankles, staring at her like he'd never seen a woman cry before. Denison and the rest of the crew, all but Connor, stood just inside the doorway, looking haunted.

"We thought someone was hurting you," Tagan said, his voice a soft stroke against her ear.

How did she explain that someone *was* hurting her? All the time.

"She's okay," he told his crew. "Go on back to bed. I'll watch her until she falls asleep."

Kellen squeezed her ankle under her flannel pajama bottom pants and gave a sad smile. It should've felt too intimate coming from a stranger, but instead, a comforting warmth spread up her leg. Denison stepped forward and brushed his fingertips over her head, and the same warm tendrils flooded her, making her feel dizzy, like she'd taken a cheap shot of whiskey. The other men did the same, one by one.

"Why did they do that?" she asked when they had gone.

Tagan slid his arm under the crease behind her knees and lifted her onto the bed. "Because touch is important to us. You were hurt. None of them would've been able to sleep tonight if they didn't reassure themselves you were okay."

"It felt..."

A slight frown took Tagan's face. "It felt like what?"

"Comforting."

His eyebrows shot up, as if she'd caught him by surprise. Seconds ticked by as he studied her face—for what, she didn't know. "I'm going to get you a drink of water, and then we should talk about what happened to you."

Brooke lifted her chin and shook her head. "I don't want to do that—"

"But you will, or that nightmare will follow you to the grave. Wait here."

Panicked at the idea of sharing that night with anyone, she clutched the comforter and eyed the window. She could just leave. She could leave here and keep the hurt inside where it belonged.

Tagan returned, disrupting any thoughts of escape. He handed her a glass of water and turned to flip the switch on an old-fashioned sconce on the wall. The soft glow of a lightbulb bathed the room, and Brooke drew the covers over her lap like armor. No doubt her hair was a rumpled mess, and she was wearing the least attractive pajama set she'd ever laid eyes upon. It was the reason she'd bought it, so she could be invisible.

But here, in front of Tagan, with him studying her with that unsettling calmness about him, she wished she'd brought something cuter. He wore a thin, gray cotton T-shirt, still rumpled and tear-stained from her earlier meltdown. Black sweats were slung low across his tapered waist and his feet were bare as he drew one under him.

As she cradled the glass of cold water, he reached over and tugged at the bandage on her neck. The one she never removed unless she was switching it out for a new one.

She allowed it. God, she was actually going to let someone see the ugliest part of her. And not just someone, but Tagan, who felt…important.

She scrunched her face as the adhesive pulled at her skin.

"Brooke, why do you have a bandage over an injury that is healed?"

"Because it doesn't feel healed."

"It still hurts?"

"No."

Tagan folded the bandage carefully and dropped his gaze. His motions were slow, calculated. "What happened?"

Tagan thought she was weak. She saw it when he'd helped rid her trailer of the mouse, and she could see it now. But she wanted to be stronger. She wanted his respect. Tilting her chin up and straightening her spine, she said, "I was mugged. He was caught. He went to jail for three months, and now he's free. I left Boulder because I wanted to get better."

He huffed air from his lungs and dragged his gaze to hers. His eyes were such a strange color. Blue and green and brown all at once. Churning, as if something she'd said had angered him. "That's a nice, shortened version there, but that won't help you deal with this, and it won't help me understand." He patted the bed and settled a pillow, then lay beside it, hands hooked behind his head. "I've got all night."

With a long, steadying sigh, she lay beside him on the pillow he'd fluffed for her and stared at the sagging ceiling. "I was a painter. I had shows in galleries and made a living off my art. People wanted to be near me and speak with me about how I created and why. I had everything. Friends, a supportive family, a mentor who was with me every step of the way. My apartment wasn't the nicest, but it was home, and soon, I was going to have enough money saved up to buy a condo I'd been eyeing. My life was perfect."

"Nobody's life is perfect."

"Mine was." She saw it now, that perfect life dancing just out of her reach. Days filled with outings to appease her creative side, and nights spent in her studio, working out everything she wanted to say with oils or acrylics. When she became too comfortable with one, she switched.

Stacks of blank canvases, waiting for her to put a story on them. Waiting to be hung in the galleries who were happy to provide space and good lighting for her when she had enough to sell. Champagne and pictures for local newspapers, and Meredith always there when her nerves got the best of her.

"I like to take the stairs instead of the elevator. Elevators have always scared me. Probably because when I was younger, my mom and I got stuck on one for a few hours. I was a creature of habit, always leaving around the same time to go to the gym or to go pick up food. A man stopped me and asked me for a light in one of the wells one night, but I didn't think anything of it. I told him I didn't smoke and went on my way. The next day, he was there again, but instead of a light, he wanted my purse this time." Thickness clogged her throat as she thought about how mad the man had been when she fumbled. "I tried to hand my purse to him, but it was a small one with a wrist strap, and when it didn't slide off, I yanked to try and loosen it. Only, it came out of the man's hand instead. He hit me." She pitched her voice to nothing but a whisper. "I thought he would kill me, but he only laughed when I pleaded with him not to. He gave me the mark because he wanted me to remember what he'd done and how helpless I really am. He made the mark with a pocket knife. I don't wear the bandage because it hurts, Tagan. I wear it so I don't see how pathetic I am in the mirror every day."

"What's his name?"

"Doesn't matter."

"Does to me." His voice sounded grittier than she'd heard before, and when he spoke, the air in the room felt heavy, harder to breathe.

She wanted to give him what he demanded, really, but thinking about saying that monster's name out loud felt like conjuring the devil himself. "I can't."

His body went rigid beside her. "You aren't pathetic, Brooke. And you aren't weak."

"You thought I was. I could tell when you saw me

scream at that mouse."

"I was wrong. You're maybe the bravest woman I've ever met."

Those words. Oh, what they did to her heart. A layer of loneliness slipped from her, making her feel raw and exposed, but hopeful, too.

"What happened to your paintings?" He rested his arm by her side and squeezed her hand gently with his.

Flutters filled her stomach as he left his warm hand on top of hers. The callouses on his palm rubbed against the smoothness of her hand. They really were from two different worlds, but everything in her sang that Tagan knew heartache, too. He was a kindred spirit who would understand, if only she could be brave enough to explain.

"I can't paint anymore. Every time I try, it comes out dark. Different. Unsellable. The bright parts of me that created before were snuffed out. I guess...I guess I came out here because I thought I could connect to the outdoors and find my muse again."

"You drew starscapes." It wasn't a question, but a statement.

"Yes."

"Put your jacket on." He sat up and scrubbed both hands down his face. His hair was still mussed from sleep, but when he looked back at her, his expression wasn't tired. It was kind. Her fingers twitched for the warmth he'd taken with him when he'd let go of her hand, but in this moment, she knew exactly what Tagan was.

He was a friend. He was a decent person. And he was a good man.

And as scary as it was to trust someone with her darkest secrets, he wasn't running. This perfect stranger was offering her sanctuary she hadn't known existed.

Five minutes later, teeth brushed, jeans and sweater on, jacket folded over her arm, Brooke waited on her porch for Tagan. She hadn't known which trailer he lived in, but one across the road and two down had the light on. When Tagan ducked under the front door and smiled at her, all doubt was erased. A strange zing of excitement traveled up her spine that he lived so close.

With a silent twitch of his chin, he gestured her to follow. She jogged to catch him, pulling on her jacket as she ran. It was still winter, but on the cusp of spring, and even though the days were warm, the nights had a chill that bit right through those trailer walls. She'd been sleeping with the window unit heater blasting and still hadn't managed to keep the gooseflesh off her calves.

The light from the park disappeared as Tagan opened a gate for her and waited for her to pass.

"It's so dark," she whispered, afraid to wake the others. If she could hear every word through the walls of her rental, surely they could, too.

"I figured you'd have trouble seeing," Tagan said, handing her a cold, black cylinder. "Here."

Brooke clicked on the flashlight and pointed it toward the ground. "And you don't have trouble seeing in the dark?"

A simple "no" sounded over his broad shoulder before he marched off at a grueling pace.

The trail wound this way and that like some giant serpent through the trees. The smell of pine was fragrant, and the sound of forest birds soft in the distance. Gentle wind rocked the branches in the evergreen canopy over their heads, and the pine needles made swishing sounds as she walked across them.

"Where are you taking me?" she asked, desperate to fill the silence. The dark had frightened her as a child, and out here in the middle of nowhere, those fears crept back.

"You'll see."

She halted. "I don't know about this. I think we should go back. It's the middle of the night."

"You scared?" he asked. It wasn't a taunt. She could tell when he turned around. In the illumination of the flashlight, his expression only held concern.

Embarrassed, and afraid her voice would shake, she nodded her head.

"Of me?"

"No." She frowned. By all accounts, she had every right to be afraid of him. She'd only met him yesterday and was in the woods with him, in complete darkness, and no one knew where she was. But for whatever reason, instinctual perhaps, Tagan didn't feel like a threat to her. Instead, he made her feel...safe.

He approached slowly arms extended, but didn't touch her, as if he were trying to calm a frightened animal. "It's five minutes more hiking, and we'll be there. You shared something big with me tonight, and

I know that was hard. I'm sharing something of mine, too."

A slow smile stretched her face. "Something special?"

His Adam's Apple bobbed as he swallowed hard. "Yes."

Something flashed, and she jerked the beam of light toward it. "What was that?"

Tagan's warm palm pushed her hand down, and softly, he pressed her thumb against the button that turned the flashlight off. "Look," he said, so close his chest pressed against her shoulder blades, and his breath tickled her ear.

A tiny glow shone then disappeared. Another followed, farther away and to the left. Then another and another.

"They're fireflies," Tagan explained in a hushed tone. "They stay active late into the night up here."

She'd seen fireflies before, but not like this. As more and more lit up, she gasped. "They're beautiful."

Tagan looked down at her, holding her gaze in the soft moonlight. "Yeah. Beautiful."

Her heart beat against her chest as his eyes dipped to her lips. Her breath froze in her chest as he leaned closer.

"You want me to kiss you, don't you?" he asked low.

The fireflies illuminated the woods behind him with their twinkling lights. Her lips throbbed with wanting, and her chest stirred like she was just coming back to life after a long slumber. If he kissed her, she'd be changed from the inside out. From her cells to her muscle fibers to her pounding heart, everything would be different. She wanted that. She wanted to live again.

Searching his eyes, she nodded. "Yes."

His chin tilted slightly, and he gave her a hard look. "You're too good for this place. You shouldn't be wanting things like that."

He pulled away and turned his back on her. Not before she saw something dark in his eyes. Hurt, or perhaps regret, she wasn't sure.

Angry and feeling tricked, she clenched her hands at her sides and glared at his receding back. "I shouldn't want things like what? To kiss a man? I didn't ask you to get that close to me. You leaned in, and now you're shaming me for *feeling*?"

"No, Brooke," he said, turning, "you should

absolutely want to kiss a man. Try saving your affection for someone who returns it next time."

Her mouth dropped open. How utterly confusing. She'd completely misread that moment with the fireflies, and now she'd angered him. Admittedly, she didn't have that much experience with the opposite sex. Still, his abruptness stung. "I'm sorry I..." She didn't know what she was supposed to apologize for. Clearly, she'd done something wrong, but she hadn't a clue as to what.

He hiked up the trail, much faster than she could keep up with, and when he was nearly out of sight in her flashlight beam, he stopped and pointed to a clearing on the side of the mountain. "Here. This is where you'll get the best cell phone reception."

Confusion engulfed her as she paused beside him. "Thank you," she murmured softly, trying to keep the tremble from her voice.

"Can you see the trail we came up?"

She pointed the flashlight down the steep embankment along a thin, worn path. "Yes."

"Good. That'll lead you right back to the park."

"Where are you going?"

"Home." But he didn't go back down the trail.

Instead, he disappeared into the woods.

"What did I do wrong?" she blurted out.

Tagan didn't answer. Hell, from the way he'd torn out of there, he was probably too far away to hear her. A stupid, treacherous tear slipped down her cheek, and she dashed it away angrily. She'd trusted Meredith to rent a decent place for her. This trip hadn't been her idea. It had been her mentor's. *Let me take care of everything*, she'd said. Yeah, well look where that got her. Then she'd been stupid enough to trust Tagan, a complete stranger, and a man so hot and cold she couldn't read his mood from one moment to the next. And now he'd abandoned her out here in the woods in the middle of the freaking night. She was pretty sick and tired of trusting others, only to be left on her ass.

Another tear came, and another. And just in case that jerk Tagan was watching her from the woods somewhere, she turned her back to the forest and looked out over the valley between this mountain and the next.

"Oh, my gosh," she whispered as her gaze landed on the starry night before her.

A million specks of light pierced the dark veil

above her. The mountains were only dark shadows, tinged in the blue moonlight, but the stars...the stars were resplendent.

Brooke sagged to her knees at the grandeur of it all. No city lights tainted the sky here. There was just wilderness as far as the eye could see, and millions upon millions of stars.

Her soul opened like the blossom of a spring flower as she relaxed under the dark blanket of the sky. She let the breeze have her neck as she stretched her head back to see everything above her.

One last tear streamed down her face, but this one wasn't from anger or confusion. It was from reverence. Leaning backward until she lay on the ground, she spread her hands and ankles out and inhaled deeply.

Tagan had said this place was where the best reception was, but that wasn't why he'd brought her up here. He'd brought her here to loosen her muse, because on some level, he'd known what she needed. And it was this, right here. Moments of silence with the thing she'd adored painting for so long.

"I think you should stay," Tagan said from right behind her.

She should've been startled, but oddly enough, she was getting used to the silent way he and his crew moved.

"I thought you hated me."

"I don't hate you, Brooke," he said, lowering himself until he lay beside her. "I just can't get involved with you like that. I don't do one night stands."

"Me either. I'm sorry I pushed you too far. I just haven't been around a man like you. I got lost in the moment." She shook her head self-consciously and thanked the heavens above that Tagan couldn't see the heat burning across her cheeks.

"I was going to leave, but I saw you. You dropped to your knees when you saw the stars. You cried."

Embarrassment flooded her face with fire until the tips of her ears burned. That had been a private moment, not meant for his eyes. "I thought you left."

"I know what you're thinking. You think I'll see you as weak for crying, but I don't. I already told you that. You dropped to your knees, and that's what I did when I saw this place three months ago. It touched you. I don't know how to fix what's been broken with your paintings, but I have a feeling this place is a start. I don't want you to go in the morning. I think you owe it to yourself to see this thing through." He turned his face until his eyes met hers. "I think you're meant to be here."

She dabbed moisture from the corner of her eye with her coat sleeve and dragged her gaze back up to the glittering sky above them. "Maybe you're right. I do feel different here. I've been in a rut for so long, it's nice to feel something new."

"So you'll stay?"

Stay in that tiny trailer in a park full of sweaty lumberjacks? She hadn't considered it before, but she also hadn't seen this place. And she hadn't spent time with Tagan. Oh, she'd heard him loud and clear when he'd said he didn't have affection for her like that. But there was something about him—something that called to her and told her that her life would be lacking if she didn't get to know him better.

In one night with Tagan, her heart had been ripped opened and bled slowly with the awful memories of the man who'd hurt her. She'd been tossed this way and that on the tidal waves of her emotions. But at least she felt something. For months, she'd been numb, but tonight, she felt that spark in her chest again.

She shook her head in disbelief and sighed. "I'll stay."

FIVE

Tagan couldn't throw the truck into park fast enough.

"Don't worry," Kellen said from the passenger's seat. "Your mate's still here."

Tagan graced his best friend with an exasperated look. "Would you stop calling her that, man? Rein in the heavy bear shifter shit. She's not like us. You have to knock it off, at least until she leaves. She's not my mate."

"Your face just went all sad when you talked about her leaving." Kellen shoved the door open and slid out of the work truck. "She's your mate."

"The fuck she is," Connor called from his position leaning on the railing of his front porch.

Tagan stifled the growl that threatened to rattle his throat. Connor, that dick, had probably spent his entire day off pestering Brooke while Tagan was up in the mountains, cutting lumber, stripping logs, loading trucks, and going crazy with the thought of that rangy shifter anywhere near her.

"We're just friends," he muttered. The snarling animal inside of him thoroughly disagreed.

Brooke's car wasn't in front of her trailer, and a flood of panic constricted Tagan's insides. He jogged toward 1010. "Where is she?" he asked Connor.

"Looks like you ran her off," Connor said through a smirk.

If anyone ran her off, it was that asshole, and if he did, Tagan was going to bleed him. He needed more time with her. Not to claim her. Just to...aw fuck, who was he kidding? He wanted her bad. His bear wanted her worse. She was all long blond hair, eyes the color of honey, and petite—the perfect size for protecting. He could make every excuse in the book to kick her out of here, but after last night, he hadn't been able to stand the thought of her leaving and not learning more about her.

He bounded up her stairs two at a time and threw open the front door. *Please, please let her stuff still be in here.* He bolted for the bedroom and gripped the door frame until it creaked. Rolling his eyes back in his head, he sighed with relief at the sight of her suitcase and unmade bed. He didn't know her that well, but Brooke didn't strike him as a person who'd leave without making the bed.

Paper fluttered from somewhere in the trailer, brushing soft noises against his oversensitive eardrums. What was that?

He strode back across the living room to the second bedroom on the other side and stopped short when he reached the open door.

Sheets of oversize paper littered the floor, each painted with an image of the same man's face. One sat half-finished and clipped to an easel. Tagan knelt down and raised the closest of the discarded pieces to the window light.

Cold, empty eyes, staring straight ahead...no...straight through him. It was painted in dark colors, and the only highlights were where she'd left the cream-colored paper raw and untouched. The only color other than black was the gray in his eyes.

He looked around. She had used the same gray in all of the paintings. Some were of the man snarling his lip or looking down. In one, he was laughing, but the smile looked cruel.

Slow rage built inside of Tagan, small and unassuming at first, then bigger and brighter, until the animal inside of him threatened to shred him from the inside out.

He hunched forward, crumpling the man's picture in his fists.

He'd hurt Brooke, this monster.

"Not here," Kellen said softly from behind. "You can't tear up her home, Tagan. She feels safe here, but she won't if she sees an animal has ripped up her place."

Kellen was right. Dammit, he was always right. Right and level-headed, and it was Kellen who should've been Second in the clan. He just hadn't been interested. Not like Tagan and Connor had been. Chest heaving against the urge to Change, Tagan loosened his grip on the painting. Seconds dragged on as he fought his animal for his skin. His muscles were so tight, it was hard to move, hard to think. Teeth gritted, he forced his hands open and rested his palms on the cool, laminate flooring.

Breath. Just breathe. She's not gone. She's here. Away from that asshole who hurt her. She's safe...with me.

Safe with him? He was losing his mind.

"Where is she?" Tagan's voice came out low and gravelly, inhuman.

"Connor said she went into town for groceries," Kellen said. "She probably got tired of him harassing her all day." Kellen cleared his throat and knelt down to run his finger across an angry looking red slash mark across one of Brooke's paintings. "Connor is going to cause trouble for you. And for her. You realize that, right?"

"I can handle Connor."

"Mmm," Kellen said, noncommittally.

Heaving a sigh, Tagan leaned back on his heels and stared helplessly across the room of paintings. Paintings Brooke had created out of the pain churning inside of her. She was scared of being seen as weak—ridiculous woman. She was hiding all of this from the world. His stomach clenched in on itself just thinking about the monumental effort she must put forth everyday just to appear normal. He'd give anything to take this pain away from her, to have saved her from that experience in the stairwell—the one that made her run into the wilderness to try to feel safe and whole again.

His mate was fierce. His mate was stronger than anyone he'd ever met. She was still getting up every day, trying to fight her fear and heal her scars, and if it was the last thing he did, he was going to show her just how powerful she was.

His mate? Shit.

A long, contented rumble left Tagan's throat, and Kellen smiled like he knew everything that ever was. Tagan needed out of this place. He needed to see Brooke, to reassure his bear that she wasn't gone forever, just for now.

He needed to make sure she was safe and whole, not just for her, but for selfish reasons. He had to convince himself she was okay so he could calm the rage that had ignited in his gut, then settled into a discomfort that wouldn't go away.

He was sweaty and filthy from working the landing all day, but that didn't stop him from jumping behind the wheel of his truck and blasting out of the trailer park. Connor watched him go with narrowed, accusing eyes, but Tagan didn't give a shit. Brooke was his, but he'd be damned if he hurt her more by claiming her. He cared about her enough to be her friend and let her go. Oh, he'd pine for her always after she left, but he'd be justified in his decision. She'd go back to her life, and he'd hope she looked back on her time here fondly. His bear had chosen her, and she'd always stick. It was how it was with shifters. He'd give her up, though, because he refused to hurt her. Not like that man in the stairwell.

As soon as he was in range of good reception, he pressed the only speed dial he had programmed into his cell phone.

"I was wondering when you were going to call," Meredith said into the phone. Even from hundreds of miles away, he could tell she was smiling as she spoke. He could hear it in her voice.

"It's been a long time, Mom."

"Too long. I hear you have been taking good care of my girl. She called me an hour ago. Gave me an earful about my rental mistake but admitted she is going to stay for a while. You must have charmed her well."

Tagan gripped the steering wheel and glared at the gravel road that was disappearing under his tires. "Why did you send her here?"

His mother's answer was simple. "Because you need each other."

He bit back a curse because she had always been a right proper lady and hated when his foul mouth ran away with him. His knuckles were turning white from his strangle hold on the wheel. "Right. And when she leaves me, and I feel like my life isn't fulfilling anymore, like I can't be happy anymore and my bear is out of control, what then?"

"I don't know, son," she said softly. "I just know that I've watched her for years. Seen her grow up as an artist, and everything she does complements who you are."

Tagan pinched the bridge of his nose and sighed a long, steadying breath. "The man who hurt her…"

"You don't have to worry about him."

"Brooke said he got out of jail—"

"Tagan," his mom said carefully, then repeated slowly, "You don't have to worry about him."

Tagan nodded. He knew exactly what she was

saying. She'd probably killed the man in some back alley, claws out as she let him see his doom before it came. That she had avenged Brooke said everything about how important she was to Mom.

"Okay," he drawled, his bear settling by a fraction. The threat to Brooke was over, and he wouldn't have to travel to kill her attacker.

"I knew he was getting out," she said, "but couldn't make a move until Brooke was out of the city and away from it all. His death couldn't blow back on her, you understand?"

He did. His mother was a momma bear and protector, down to the core, and an intelligent hunter. That man had conjured the wrath of an apex predator the second he marked Brooke's neck. Jail had only prolonged his life.

"Has she painted anything yet?" Mom asked.

"Yeah, but I think she's worse off than ever. There are two dozen paintings of her attacker's face she must've done this morning."

"Good."

"Good? They aren't exactly the pretty star paintings she talks about wanting to get back to. They're full of pain and grit and…" Fuck, his bear was doubling him over the wheel just thinking about it.

"But she's painting. She hasn't been able to do that in three months. When someone like Brooke loses their creative outlet, all of that energy doesn't just leave her. It's still there, trapped and turning poisonous by the day. If she needs to paint her anger, fine. At least it's a start. This is something she needs. She needs to work through this, or it could ruin her, Tagan. Not just her ability to make a living, but it could ruin her creativity. Turn it black and untrustworthy. Even from his grave, that criminal could take away her livelihood. Tagan," she said, voice stony. "Don't let that happen."

The line went dead.

Tagan flipped the phone onto the passenger's seat and scrubbed his free hand over his two-day stubble. He could barely keep his crew from tearing each other's throats out when Jed was away, and now Brooke's happiness rested on his shoulders? What if he screwed this up? What if she ended up hating him because of it? What if he pushed too hard, and she lost her love of painting completely?

He knew exactly how important muses were. He'd been raised by an artist, after all. The urge that lived inside of Brooke, the one that told her she must *create*, was just as important as her talent to do so.

He hit the gas as he blasted past a green sign that informed him Saratoga was twenty-five miles away.

Whatever he had to do to help Brooke get her life back, he'd do it.

SIX

Brooke eyed the fabric swatches in the home improvement aisle at the general store on the main drag in town. It only sold two shades of blackout curtains, sky blue and sunny yellow.

She'd had big plans to sleep in this morning after the late night she'd kept, but the blaring sunlight in her bedroom had other ideas. Her eyelids were probably sunburned from her attempt to ignore it. And then, out of frustration, she'd woken up and did something awful. Painted something awful. Lots of somethings.

She'd never actually felt pain when she was painting before, but this morning, she'd almost made herself sick with the images of her attacker that flowed from her paintbrush and onto those canvases.

She snatched a couple of packaged curtains in blue and tossed them into the cart. She made to speed off toward the art supplies section but pulled the cart to a stop and stared thoughtfully at a shelf of bathmats. A gold one kind of matched the baby-diarrhea-colored bathtub. She grabbed that and took another look down the aisle. It was kind of fun shopping for her trailer, now that she was going to stay for a while. A kitchen mat, a towel set for the bathroom, a miniature wicker trashcan, and a pair of soap dispensers later, Brooke was looking forward to decorating her little place. It had already been furnished when she came, but the little personal touches were missing. And the more she found enjoyment out of picking out those personal touches, the more 1010 felt like a home away from home.

With her bags in hand, she stepped out of the general store and waved to an older man in coveralls who waved back. Without her asking, he grabbed the heavy bags and walked her to her car, chatting about the weather and how it was supposed to rain tomorrow. She thanked him, and he tipped his ball cap and went on his way, but she stood there for a minute, watching him leave. That was the first time anyone had offered to help her with her bags, and he was a complete stranger.

She looked down Bridge Avenue and smiled at the hustle and bustle of the town's residents after getting off work. A number of restaurants seemed to be drawing in the crowds, but even the busiest passersby nodded their heads in greeting. She liked this place. Everyone seemed friendly. This was different from the city where she sometimes felt like a number in the masses.

She locked up her car and jogged across the street to a small grocery store. She'd been too stubborn to beg breakfast off Connor this morning, and now she was starving. Intending to fully stock the small swing-door pantry in 1010 and fill the fridge, she pulled the door open and grabbed a cart.

Shopping on an empty stomach was a terrible idea. She wanted every food she passed by. The basket was already half full by the time she stopped in front of the cold cuts in the back.

Steak, yes.

Pork chops, absolutely.

Bacon? Hell yes to that. She had a craving, and it involved copious amounts of the savory strips of meat.

Someone ran into her cart with theirs, and the sound of metal on metal nearly made her jump out of her skin.

"Hey there, stranger," Tagan said through a cocky grin. "Fancy meeting you here."

His bright blue eyes held her trapped, her body locked against any movement. He'd filled her mind all day, but was the last person she'd expected to see here. "H-hi."

His grin deepened. "You planning on eating all that bacon yourself?"

She stifled a smile, because really the man shouldn't be encouraged. "Are you judging my groceries?"

"You don't want to cook bacon in a trailer."

"I want a BLT."

"What's that?" he asked, leaning on the front handle of his cart. His muscles looked yummy all flexed like that, and when his T-shirt stretched farther up his arm, a small tendril of ink was exposed on his tricep. A tattoo? Dammit, she was a sucker for those.

"Brooke? You okay?"

With a monumental effort, she dragged her gaze back to his and cleared her throat. "I'm fine." Except her voice had gone up an octave. She cleared her throat again and tried to mentally stifle the burning heat that was creeping up her neck. "Bacon, lettuce, and tomato."

His dark eyebrows drew down. "Pardon?"

"A BLT. It's a bacon, lettuce, and tomato sandwich. Put them on some toasted bread with mayo and bingo bango, magic in your mouth."

His eyes dipped to her lips, and the heat in her cheeks flamed hotter.

A knowing smile crooked those sexy lips of his, and he pulled his attention back to the refrigerated shelf of meat. The grin slowly faded. "I have to tell you something."

"Okay." That sounded foreboding.

"I saw those paintings you did this morning."

Horror slammed into her middle. Gripping the bar of her cart, she gritted her teeth to stifle the urge to verbally filet him right here in front of the meandering shoppers. "You had no right to go into my place."

"Yeah, I did," he said, the humor gone from his voice. "I thought maybe you left. I was making sure your stuff was still in there."

His tone sounded hurt, and her ready insults froze on her tongue.

"Now, listen before you get on me, woman. I'm not good at talking, and I don't say the right things most of the time, so bear with me. That's not all I wanted to tell you." He stopped, searching her eyes like he didn't know how to go on.

"What else, then?" she asked, scared of what he would say but too curious to let him go without attempting.

"I'm proud of you."

Whatever she'd thought was going to come out of that man's mouth, that wasn't it. "What? Why?"

He drew up close to her, close enough to touch and lowered his voice. "I know it cost you to start painting again, especially like that. I'm proud you're facing your demons, Brooke."

"You don't think..." How could she ask his

opinion without seeming needy? How did she tell him his thoughts on her work meant more than the art critic's write-ups in her local newspaper? How could she stand here, looking at this almost stranger, and tell him his views on those paintings, the ones she planned on never showing anyone, meant the world to her? "Do you think I'm crazy now?"

"Because of what I saw in those paintings? No. I think you're hurt, and I think that asshole deserved to be painted like you did. I didn't like the subject of them, but anyone with eyes in their head can see you are an artist, and a good one at that. Keep painting that man, or paint stars or horses or jack-a-lopes, I don't care. I just think it's good that you're painting."

Pride surged through her, spreading outward from her middle until she was warmed with it. He got it. This man who worked with his hands all day. This man who was caked in dirt, contrasting against the clean, white linoleum tiles beneath their feet. This rough-around-the-edges, tatted-up country boy understood her in a way no one ever had before, and perhaps in a way no one ever would again.

"It means a lot that you said that," she admitted quietly. Without thinking, she reached forward and brushed a spot of dried mud off his forearm. His muscles bunched and tensed, startling her, and when she glanced up, he looked just as rocked as she felt. Holding her breath, she rested the palm of her hand against his arm and left it there, daring him to jerk away from her. He didn't. Instead, he pulled her other hand to his lips, and brushed a light kiss across her knuckles. His eyes were so intense, they almost seemed to change colors in the fluorescent lighting. His lips were soft against her skin as he lingered there. "We're friends," he said, dropping her hands gently to her sides. "Touch me like that, and I'll want more." It sounded like a threat the way he said it.

Without another word, he pushed his cart forward and left her there, knees unsteady and warmth pooling between her legs.

She stared at the small mountain of bacon in her cart with wide eyes and rubbed her tingling knuckles where he'd kissed them.

He made it sound like a bad thing, him wanting more, but to her, it sounded just right.

****

Brooke parked in front of her trailer and stared out the side window in disbelief. Bruiser leaned against the fence near the front entry sign watching Denison glide over a gravelly clearing behind a white, jacked-up monster truck. Haydan, Drew, and Kellen were hootin' and hollerin' from the bed of the truck while Connor was driving donuts on what looked like an old, oversize basketball court.

"Is Denison skiing?" she asked as she approached.

"They found a pair in the storage closet in the office," Bruiser said, bending at the waist until he rested his weight onto the rickety, splintered fence.

From here, she could make out the skis on Denison's feet as he held onto a rope. Sparks were flying from the backs of the skis. "Aren't they worried about starting a fire?"

"Nah, it's too wet. Won't catch."

She giggled as Denison wobbled.

"Straighten out, you pussy!" Haydan yelled, then they all burst out laughing as Connor jerked the wheel, and Denison flew sideways, losing control.

He landed hard in the grass, but none of them even waited to see if he was okay before Drew was out of the truck and pulling the skis off Denison's feet. "My turn," he declared.

By the time all of the men had a turn, Brooke was nearly crying with laughter. As she wheezed and doubled over, Bruiser clapped her on the back and boomed a laugh right along with her.

"Idiots," he said, wiping moisture from the outside corners of his eyes.

"They're lucky none of them were seriously hurt," Brooke said. She had a cramp in her side from laughing and massaged it with her fingers.

"It'd take much more than that to injure a—" Bruiser jerked his gaze to hers and the smile dropped from his face. He cleared his throat. "You got groceries you need help carrying in?"

Brooke canted her head and frowned. "To injure a what?"

"What?"

"That's what I'm asking. You said it would take much more to injure, then you let it drop. Injure a what, Bruiser?"

"Man with that many beers in his system. Come on." The humor in his face was gone as he turned and marched away.

She followed slowly. That wasn't what he was about to say. "What's going on?" she asked.

Bruiser ignored her and jogged to her car, as if attempting to escape her questions.

"Fine. Keep your stupid secrets."

"Tagan's planning a celebration for you tonight." Bruiser pulled open the back door to her car and tugged out a couple of shopping bags.

Brooke locked her legs and skidded to a stop. "A celebration for what?" Please, God, don't let it be for painting again. Her issues were not something she wanted to make public knowledge here.

"It's a welcome to the park celebration. At least, that's what he said on the phone. He's picking up supplies in town for a barbecue. You'll die and go straight to heaven when you taste the food tonight."

He was distracting her, but okay. It was better than awkward silence. "Oh. Well, is there anything I can bring?"

"Just yourself. You're queen of this place now. Let us spoil you like good old boys know how."

A grin cracked her face, and she ducked her chin before he could see it. Maybe Connor had been right to call her princess. She was a trailer park princess now. Her friends back home would crap themselves if they knew how happy she was in this place. It was the first time in months she'd been able to smile without feeling some awful sense of guilt. Here, the troubles of the city seemed far away.

Bruiser did most of the heavy lifting with her groceries and art supplies, and when she went out to check that they hadn't missed a bag, she noticed Brighton hauling heavy-looking metal buckets of water over to the back of his truck. The weight looked substantial, but it didn't seem to slow him down one little bit. The edges of a blue tarp flapped in the wind over the sides of the truck bed, so she meandered over there to see what he was doing. Bruiser followed.

"What are you doing?" she asked Brighton.

The man didn't talk, but his animated expressions conveyed complete thoughts. The twinkle in his eyes was downright naughty, and he twitched his head toward the blue tarp that lined the bed completely. It was already holding water, and when he dumped the huge vats of hot water into it, the surface began to steam.

"Did you make a hot tub?"

Brighton nodded slowly and twitched his head toward the back again.

"You want me to go swimming?" she asked.

He nodded and grinned like he was daring her.

She looked at the steaming water again, then back to Brighton to gauge if he was joking. It was obvious he thought she'd say no, and something about that bothered her.

"I'll put my swimsuit on."

Bruiser chuckled, and Brighton's eyebrows arched in surprise.

She bit back the smile as she jogged back to her trailer. Thank goodness, she'd decided to shave this morning. It wasn't easy either. There were only five minutes of hot water in 1010, and she had shaved at the speed of light. She had three cuts to show from her Olympic-style razor race, too, but hey, at least she was smooth for the little two-piece she'd brought in case the "fancy rental" had a pool.

She changed in record time and slipped into a pink fuzzy robe and glittery black flip flops, then speed-walked back to Brighton's truck.

Brighton was already lounging in the hillbilly hot tub, and Bruiser was leaning against the back of the truck, talking animatedly with a beer in his hand. "You want one?" he asked as she approached.

"Brooke's a lady," Kellen said as he came around the other side. "She doesn't want a beer." He hauled a giant box of wine on top of the truck and poured her a glass of sweet red into a Dixie cup.

She would've rather had the beer, but she smiled her thanks and took the wine. And after the first few sips, it wasn't that bad. God, they were so cute. It was funny seeing what these gruff men thought ladies wanted and needed. These big burly guys were killing her with how sweet they could be.

"Here, let me," Tagan said from behind her, so close, she could feel his breath on her ear. She jumped, but relaxed as he pulled the robe from her shoulders, then offered his hand to help her into the back of the truck.

His hungry eyes ravished her slowly, and an approving smile ghosted his lips. "Damn, girl."

It shouldn't have sounded like a compliment, but the way he said it, her confidence surged. Kicking off her flip flops, she lowered into the make-shift hot tub with Brighton. Dear goodness, it felt so good on her stiff muscles. Her body hadn't been acclimatized to hiking through the woods like she had last night, but this made up for it.

She almost spit out a gulp of boxed wine when she saw what Kellen was propping up on the side of Brighton's mobile home. One of her paintings had been stapled to an old board of plywood.

"What are you doing?" Her voice was pitched high. "That's my painting."

"And it's a really good painting," Tagan said. "I mean, it's amazing."

The men around her agreed, mumbling and nodding their heads.

"The man in the painting is a dick face, though. Here." Tagan handed her a set of worn darts.

She stared in horror at the sharp metal glistening in the setting sun and the fragile red and blue flights attached to the ends, shaking in the breeze. "What do you want me to do with these?"

Tagan jerked his head toward the oversize painting. It was one she'd done in black and white with a red slash mark across the middle of her attacker's face. "There's your board, Brooke. Dart the shit out of that douche-wagon so we can have a turn."

Connor came sailing over the edge of the bed, splashing them all, and Haydan, Denison, and Bruiser followed. The tub was getting ridiculously crowded, but they didn't seem to care. They splashed and laughed, all shirtless and layered with muscle. She heaved a sigh, disturbed that apparently the whole damned trailer park knew about Markus Sanger, the evil man who ruined her life. The moment should've felt serious and suffocating, but instead, the rough-housing and chaos around her took the sting off her painting on display.

"Like this," Denison said, pulling a dart from her outstretched palm.

He chucked it at the board and hit Markus right in the emotionless eye. She had to admit, it did feel nice seeing it there, hanging out of his pupil.

"I've never thrown a dart before," she admitted.

"Stand up," Tagan said without hesitation.

Unsteadily, she did as she asked, the waves from the others lapping against her calves. Tagan pulled his shirt over his head, exposing the tattoo that had peeked out from under his sleeve earlier. It was an intricate tribal rendition of some sort of large animal. A bear, perhaps.

He was all cut biceps and rippling abs, and perfect strips of muscle arced over his hip bones. Curious scars covered his defined pecs, and Brooke had to make an effort to clack her mouth closed. Holy hell balls, Tagan was ripped.

Kellen was passing out beers to the boys, so thankfully they didn't seem to notice her body was practically begging her to tackle the man. He pulled himself up on the oversized wheel and waded through the water until he stood just behind her, jeans still on and clinging just right to his lean legs.

"Like this," he said, wrapping her fingers around the dart. "Bring it back here, then let it go here."

She did and the dart arced through the air and bounced off the board.

"Good. Harder, and you would've been right where you want to be." Tagan leaned over her shoulder, and his eyes became hard, fierce. "Let that fucker have it, Brooke."

Wide-eyed, she swiveled her head back to the painting. Clenching her teeth in determination, she drew back and threw it as hard as she could. The dart landed on Markus's nose.

"Ha!" she crowed, then covered her mouth.

"Yes!" Kellen said approvingly.

"Good, woman," Tagan said, his voice low and gravelly.

Confidence filled her chest, and she downed the Dixie cup then handed the empty to Kellen. He grinned and refilled it as she blasted another one at the board. Then another. Bruiser brought them back to her when she was out, and by the third round she felt awesome. She felt empowered. She felt relieved that all of these men here knew this man had done something awful to her, and she wasn't harboring this dirty secret anymore.

She felt free.

Her eyes filled with stinging tears as the boys cheered after every good hit she made, and when her arms sagged with the relief of it all, Tagan spun her and yanked the bandage from her neck.

"This," he said, holding up what had been hiding her scar, "is gone now. You earned that scar—survived it. Own what you lived through, Brooke."

She raked her gaze down the curious scars that crisscrossed the taut skin over his chest.

Tagan's eyes were hard and serious as he allowed her to look at him. "We all have them. Ain't no shame, woman." He nodded his chin and held out his hand. "My turn."

She gave him a grateful smile and handed him

the darts. Then she sat down and accepted the newly filled Dixie cup Kellen handed her. She cheered and drank with the rest of them as these crazy, wild men blasted darts at her attacker's image.

A week ago, if someone had told her she'd be sitting in a hillbilly hot tub with a bunch of sexy, shirtless lumberjacks, chucking darts at one of her paintings and smiling harder than she had in months, she would've told them they were crazy.

And as Tagan settled in beside her and squeezed her hand, the warm water lapping at their knees as they made room for Kellen, she looked around at all the smiling faces. At the beer bottles that tinked together when someone told a funny joke and the soaked work jeans with holes in the knees when someone stood up to take a turn at the dart board.

Brooke smiled at the importance of this moment.

Meredith had known exactly what she was doing when she sent her here.

SEVEN

"You look happy," Tagan said. He sipped his beer and watched her.

Connor watched her, too, from across the fire, but his attention seemed more possessive. She'd caught Tagan staring at her often tonight, but in his eyes, adoration pooled in the deep blue color. The man could warm her with just a look. He'd been doing it all night.

The boys were currently comparing the long arm of a machine called a processor to their dicks. The night was full of dirty jokes and laughter, but she couldn't seem to stay in the conversation anymore. Her attention kept drifting to Tagan. He'd cooked for them, then gone out of his way to make sure she had everything she needed. He didn't know it, but she'd seen him shake his head at Kellen as he prepared to offer her more boxed wine.

He wasn't controlling about it, or abrasive, and she knew if she wanted, she could have more wine. But she'd had a dizzy spell earlier, and Tagan had steadied her, looking worried, then made sure Kellen didn't pressure her to finish the box on her own. She'd sobered up over the past couple of hours, but she still wasn't ready for bed. It was late, ten o'clock at least, but it was so nice to just sit here, listening to potty talk, with the laughter of her new friends as medicine for her soul. It helped that Tagan had taken an old lawn chair right beside hers.

Brighton sat down across the fire with a beat up old guitar and started strumming a song she recognized from the radio. If she had any kind of voice, she'd hum along, but as it stood, she couldn't hold a tune. Denison, however, could.

He sang a strong, clear baritone with that thick, country accent of his, and Brooke propped her feet up on an overturned log in front of her and relaxed into her plastic chair. The boys grew quiet, settling in as Denison hit the chorus. Conversation faded to an occasional murmur as the boys nursed their beers and stared at the fire in the middle of them all. Brooke looked up to the sky, suddenly yearning to see the stars she'd seen last night. The ones that looked radiant in the mountain sky.

"You want to go up there?" Tagan asked.

Brooke rolled her head toward him and smiled. "How'd you know?"

"That place calls to me, too. You can't see it as well from here. The firelight and smoke pollute the view of the sky."

Shyness crept over her, dragging heat into her cheeks. Leaning over, she whispered into his ear. "Will you come with me?"

Tagan's breath hitched, and he hesitated before he answered. She thought he would say no, but instead, he grabbed her hand and helped her up, then led her around the outskirts of the circle.

Connor's cold eyes followed them. Brooke couldn't look away from him as the firelight reflected strangely across his face. They looked like the eyes of an animal illuminated by high beams at night on the side of the road. A chill rippled across her skin, causing a wave of gooseflesh over her arms.

"Don't mind him," Tagan said.

"You know the rules, Second," Connor said. "I challenged. You can't touch her until Jed gets back."

Tagan pressed his hand against the small of her back and guided her away from the campfire.

"Why does he call you Second? And what did he mean about he challenged you?"

"Nothing you have to worry about," Tagan said, his voice hardening.

"Okay, but you know my entire ordeal, and no one will answer my questions here. You all speak in some secret code, and I get the distinct feeling I'm the only one here who is left out of the loop."

Tagan dropped his hand from her back, and she knew she'd pushed him too far. The rest of the trip to his favorite place on the mountain was quiet. Uncomfortable quiet—the kind that pressed weight onto her shoulders and made it hard to breathe.

She came through the tree line into the mountainside clearing first. The stars were just as stunning tonight as they were last night. The wind was harsher here, and she rubbed the sleeves of her jacket to conjure warmth back into her arms.

"You're right," he said. "You told me everything, and I haven't shared much with you. It's not fair. Ask me something."

She wasn't brave enough to turn around. Not yet. Instead, she gave her question to the wind. "What does Meredith mean to you guys? Every time I've mentioned her, there is a reaction, but for the life of me, I can't tell if it's good or bad. I want to know why she sent me here. The real reason, not just the bull caka excuse she gave me over the phone."

His hands slid up her arms and rested on her shoulders where he gently squeezed. "Meredith is my mother."

"What?" she said, spinning. "Your mom? Meredith James is your mother?" She couldn't help the disbelief in her voice. She tried to find any similarity between the tall, stoic, gray-haired beauty and Tagan. "But you don't look anything like her."

He laughed a surprised sound, and it echoed off the mountains. "I took after my father." He shrugged his shoulders, as if his jacket had grown too tight. "My mom says I'm the spitting image of him."

"Where is your father? I've never seen Meredith…I mean, your mom with anyone."

"He died when I was a kid. I don't remember him."

"Oh."

Hurt slashed through his eyes in the moonlight before he composed his face again.

"Listen," she said, feeling like grit. "I'm really sorry. I didn't know. I don't remember much about my dad, either." God, she was rambling, and she definitely hadn't meant to let that little jewel slip out. "I mean, he isn't dead or anything. He's just a prick." She scrunched her nose up. "But at least I got to know him well enough when I was younger to know he's a prick. What I'm trying to say is I was raised by my step-dad. My mom married a nice man, who took me in when my mom decided to make like my real dad and bail on parenting. I'm going to stop talking now."

"I think it's cute when you get all chatty like this. I learn a lot about you. And for what it's worth, I'm sorry your real parents were pricks. Where does your step-dad live?"

"In Denver where I grew up, but sometimes when I have a show, he drives to Boulder to see it."

"He sounds like a good man. A good dad."

"He's the best." Just thinking about him spiked Brooke's emotions. If he hadn't taken her in, she didn't know where she would've ended up. Probably nowhere good. "Dad was working full-time, trying to make a life for us, and he still found time to take me to art classes after school. It's all I wanted to do was paint. He even paid my tuition to get a fine arts degree in college, even though he didn't have two pennies to rub together. And never once did he tell me I should be a doctor or lawyer or anything. He always told me I was good enough to make a career in painting if I put my heart into it. Why did Connor call you Second?" She sat on a giant, gnarled pine tree root and waited.

"Because that's what I am to our crew. Second in command."

"Who's first?"

"Jedediah Mosley. You'll meet him. We all call him Jed."

"And Connor wants to challenge you for second in the crew. What do you have to do to win?"

"Beat the shit out of him. Sorry, Brooke, but you don't want to hear about that part. Best you stay far away from that chaos when it goes down."

"What did he mean, you can't touch me?"

Tagan sat down and leaned up against the towering pine beside her. "You ask a lot of questions."

"I've been saving them up."

"Neither Connor nor I can touch you until the challenge is through. And that challenge can't happen without Jed present."

"And what if I touched you?" Her mouth had gone off on its own and gotten entirely too bold. The lingering buzz from the boxed wine was probably to blame, but tonight, she wanted to be reckless and break stupid rules made up by silly boys.

He drew his gaze slowly to her. He looked troubled and inhaled a long breath. "If you touch me, the rules go out the window for me. Know that before you start teasing, woman." His voice had gone gruff and gravelly, and she closed her eyes to fully enjoy the sound of him.

She scooted closer and poked his leg with an extended finger. "Touch." Sliding a little closer, she bumped the side of his arm with hers and said again, "Touch."

A deep chuckle rattled from his throat as he

leaned his head back against the tree and stared at the starry sky above them. "Come here." He lifted his arm over his head and drew her against his side.

Brooke hadn't realized how cold she was until his warmth blanketed her. Reveling in the feeling of utter safety, she snuggled in close.

"Touch," he whispered, looking down at her. His smile faded from his face as he watched her.

A low, vibrating sound rattled from his chest as she wrapped her arms around his taut waist. She pressed the palm of her hand against his breastbone. The sound stopped, and she frowned. "Why do you do that?"

He looked at her for a long time, as if he was debating telling her everything he'd ever known. He was right there, on the edge of admitting something important—she could feel it.

When he drew away from her touch, it cut straight to her middle. A flare of anger expanded in her chest, and she threw a leg over him and straddled him, insuring he couldn't escape.

"Brooke," Tagan said, his voice deep with warning.

"Tell me why? What does that noise mean?" She

grabbed his hands and pulled them against her hips under the waist of her jacket.

The sound rattled for a moment before he jerked his head to the side and cut it off.

She rocked closer to his hips, closer to his warmth. "Tell me what it means, and I'll let you run away from me again."

"That's not what I want." Tagan's voice sounded uncertain and lost. "I don't want to run away."

"Then why won't you look at me?"

The cords of muscle in his throat were straining with his attempt to look away from her. "Because this is a bad idea." His lips said the words, but his hands drew her waist closer, right over his rigid erection under his jeans.

"Fine," she whispered, pulling him close so that her chin rested on his shoulders. "Don't look at me, but tell me what the noise you make means when we touch."

His hands went around her, and he hugged her tightly. With a trembling sigh, he said, "The sound means I like you. It means something inside of me approves of whatever you're doing when I make it. It means I'm content and happy...with you."

"I like you," she murmured, squeezing her eyes tightly closed. If he could be brave enough to tell her such things, she could share her honest feelings as a reward for him.

Tagan eased back and held the sides of her face, then leaned his forehead against hers and closed his eyes. His breathing was ragged, unsteady. Leaning forward, he brushed his lips against hers, once, twice. Two little plucks on her lips that said he was still trying to talk himself out of going any deeper with her.

He was scared. The realization rocked her. He was just as scared of her as she was of him—of how deeply she felt for him. This was big. Important. Meredith had always said the things that scared her the most were always worth the risk.

God, she hoped she was right.

Angling her chin, she kissed him just as gently as he'd done to her. Lips moving slowly against his, she rolled her hips until she sat right in the apex he'd created by drawing his knees up behind her back.

The sound came back, throaty, content, practically a purr against the palms of her hands as she slid them down to feel. "I like that sound," she whispered, pulling away slightly. "Don't hide it from me anymore."

The noise, a low growl now that grew louder as he gripped her hips and rocked her against his erection. He opened her mouth and brushed his tongue against hers. One of his hands rubbed up her back and entwined in her hair as he pulled her closer and thrust his tongue deeper into her mouth.

Holy hell balls. She'd thought Tagan was sexy before, but this? Her insides were on fire.

He adjusted the angle of her hips, and the man hit right where her oversensitive clit was pressed against her pants. Her college boyfriend hadn't managed to find that spot in the two years they'd dated, but Tagan pressed his hand against it, as if he knew exactly what would make her come.

Tagan trailed kisses from her mouth, down her jaw, to her collarbone he exposed as he pressed her jacket and sweater to the side. "I'll keep you warm," he promised as he pushed her coat from her shoulders.

The butterflies in her stomach turned to dragons as he ran his fingertips under the hem of her shirt and up her ribcage. Up and down and back up again until a shiver of pleasure trembled up her spine.

And for some strange reason, despite the stiff wind, she was warm. Tagan was growing hotter by the minute, and now, when she pulled his sweater off and pressed her hands over his rigid pecs, he felt like a furnace.

"Told you," he said, one corner of his mouth lifting in a teasing smile.

Feeling braver than she had in months, she pulled her own sweater off and unhooked her bra. She wanted nothing more than to touch his skin with hers. She wanted to feel that burning warmth against her sensitive nipples. She wanted to burrow against him until she was part of him.

She wanted to feel safe.

Tagan's eyes went wide as she shrugged out of her bra. When he slowly lifted his hands and cupped the fullness of her breasts, she rolled her eyes back at how good his touch felt. His hands were calloused from the hard labor he did to earn his living, and it contrasted against the smoothness of her skin.

Tagan eased her forward, dipped his head, then drew her nipple into his mouth. She arched against him and cupped the back of his head. His tongue lapped at her, and she imagined what he would feel like with his head between her legs. Brooke's panties were wet by the time he moved to the next to pay her other breast the same attention.

He rolled his hips in rhythm to his sucking and she bowed against him. She'd only come with a man twice, but Tagan was about to pull an orgasm from her with his jeans on.

"Oh," she said softly as he nipped her breast gently. Her breath became ragged as tingling pressure built between her thighs. "Oh!" she said louder as the pressure threatened to spill over the edge.

Tagan yanked the button of her jeans. The zipper sounded loud against the quiet night. His hand was warm as he slid it under her panties and cupped her sex. "I wanna feel," he said in a gruff voice.

Each time she moved her hips, whimpering noises wrenched from her throat. Tagan slid his finger into her and let out a long, shuddering sigh as she bucked against his hand.

"Tagan, Tagan," she moaned. "I'm going to…" All thought left her as he pressed harder onto her clit and detonated her. The orgasm rocketed through her body, making everything clench up. Her hands in his hair. Her knees around his ribs. Her insides against his finger. He pressed his thumb to her sensitive spot, rubbed it gently, prolonging her release, as if he knew exactly what her body needed.

She kissed him while her aftershocks subsided. Kissed him until they were long gone. Kissed him until her body wanted again. "I'm on birth control," she said.

"Brooke," Tagan said, shaking his head. "It's not a good idea for me to bond to you any more than I already have."

What a strange way of putting it. Bond to her. Well, she felt bonded to him, so she understood the sentiment. "You also said it wasn't a good idea to touch you, but I have no regrets," she said through a grin as she combed her fingers through his short hair. "Besides," she said, arching her eyebrow at the long, hard, roll of his shaft pressed against the fabric of his jeans. "That looks uncomfortable, and I know what can fix it."

He searched her face. Uncertainty clouded the clear blue of his eyes, so she stood.

"I used to hate what I looked like without

clothes," she admitted. It was her deepest insecurity, and she was trusting him with it. She was giving him the power to hurt her now, to reject her, and hoping that he wouldn't. "I've only slept with boys when it was completely dark." Shame heated her cheeks as she kicked her shoes off and pushed her jeans to her ankles, then stepped out of them. "I guess right now it's still dark, but I feel stronger with you. Better with you." She pushed her panties down her legs and straightened her spine, completely vulnerable before him.

Tagan raked his hungry eyes slowly over every inch of her body. He didn't have to say a word, but the enamored way he gazed at her body was enough.

"Shit, woman. You don't play fair. We're going to hurt each other on the way out of this." He lifted his gaze to hers. His eyes were serious and hard. "Are you sure you want this? Want me?"

It sounded like he was asking so much more than just to have sex with her, and her stomach churned with the rightness of what was happening between them. She wasn't just some one night stand to him.

"I want you." She ducked her head and scrunched her nose, embarrassed at being so exposed in front of another person.

Tagan stood and shucked his pants. "Come here," he murmured. "Let me hold you."

With a conscious effort, Brooke kept her mouth from hanging open at the sight of his gloriously naked body. Adonis didn't even cut it. The man was a demigod. Muscles bulging, shaft long and thick, and that alluring tattoo dark against his pale skin. His erection stood rigid in between them, and as she stepped closer, she ran her finger down the silken skin there. His hips jerked at her touch, and a helpless-sounding noise came from him as she grabbed him at the base and pulled upward.

She felt like a goddess with him. He was strong and capable. His entire crew looked to him for leadership, and he always answered with levelheaded answers, as if nothing ever got to him. And with her, he'd been tender and caring. He hadn't run away when he found out what had scared her into the person she was now. He'd done the opposite of what she expected and soothed the fire in her blood.

Tagan was unlike any man she'd ever known.

He turned them slowly as she stroked him, until

her back was pressed on the smooth bark of a towering ash tree. He scooped up his jacket and pulled it around her shoulders. "Don't want that pretty back of yours torn up," he rumbled in a soft stroke against her ear. Pressing against her, he pulled her hand over his shoulder and around his neck, then did the same with the other. His intense gaze was different now. His eyes looked a strange color in the shadow of the tree. A trick of the night, surely.

His eyes dipped to her breasts, then back up again. "Whatever hang-ups you have with your body, you don't need them with me. You're perfect. I wouldn't change a single thing about you."

"So you aren't just dressing me in your jacket to hide me away?"

He laughed and shook his head slowly. "No." He touched her sex, sliding his fingers back and forth through the moisture he'd conjured there. "I'm saving the skin on your back. But I must admit, I like the sight of you in my clothes, so anytime you want to borrow my jacket, just ask. I'll think about this, what you're letting me do to you, anytime you wear it. Fuck, you smell good."

"I smell?"

"Yeah, *good*. I can tell how aroused you are by your scent. I like that I do that do you."

The rumbling sound was almost constant in his throat now, barely audible, but there. He nipped her lip, then ducked and grazed his teeth over her neck. A delicious shiver shook her shoulders.

A smile in his voice, Tagan said, "I like when I do that to you, too." He pressed his finger inside of her, then touched her clit until she sighed a little whimper. "And that, too. You're a noisy little thing. I like you telling me what you like. What you want."

"I want you," she said on a breath, tired of the games.

She was ready to be filled.

Ready to feel him.

Ready to be even closer to the man she was falling hard for.

"Say it again," he said, smile dipping from his face as he watched her lips.

"I want you."

His breath became uneven. Behind her knee, he lifted her leg until her hips were angled where he wanted them. "I want you, too," he whispered, teasing her opening with the head of his cock. One shallow dip, and he pulled back.

God, she was so ready for him. Stretching up, she kissed him, brushing her tongue against his in a tease of her own. The growling sound in his throat grew louder as she pressed her hips forward. His shaft sank halfway inside of her, and she moaned at how good the stretch felt.

He kissed her long and deep, massaging the back of her neck as he rocked his shaft in and out of her.

Desperate for all of him, she begged, "Please, Tagan, more."

His arms were shaking, his breath ragged, his kiss more demanding, and she could almost see his reserve dissolving. Whatever he was waiting for, she didn't need it. She didn't need a gentle man. She needed Tagan, and all the pent up desire she'd seen in his eyes all night.

"More?" he asked, bucking into, filling her completely.

"Harder," she said. Pressure, pressure, pressure, and how could a man feel this good? How could anything feel so good?

Tagan drew out slowly, then thrust into her again. He dropped her leg, gripped her hips, and drew out again. His pace picked up, and Brooke gripped his back, pulling him closer. It still wasn't enough, couldn't ever be enough. His powerful hips bucked as he pushed into her harder and faster.

The pleasure was so potent, it consumed her. She closed her eyes against the intensity. She yelled his name as her orgasm pounded through her. Tagan growled out as his warmth splashed into her, and his thrusting became erratic. He slowed and then stopped, just held her. Rocking back and forth, he kissed her forehead, her cheeks, her lips, her nose.

It was hard to stand on her wobbly legs after what they'd done. Something had changed on a cellular level inside of her. Feelings she thought she was incapable of were bubbling to the surface. Now, she was in much, much deeper with Tagan than she'd ever allow herself to admit out loud.

As minutes dragged on, Tagan grew hard and swelled inside of her again. Without a word, he gently rocked until she came again. This time wasn't rushed or desperate for release like before. This one he gave her just because he cared. He drew her orgasm from her softly and froze as she pulsed around him. Only then did he pull out of her.

Tagan picked his sweater up from the ground and turned it inside out, then knelt in front of her and brushed it across her sex and down the moisture that had trickled down her thighs.

"What are you doing?" she asked.

"Cleaning you."

"But you don't have to—"

"I want to."

"Okay," she whispered, feeling cared for and adored.

When he was done, he pulled her panties on, then her jeans, then her bra. Turning her with gentle hands, he hooked the lingerie in back, then pulled her sweater over her head.

When he was dressed, sans his shirt, which he kept clutched in his hands, he led her back down the trail, holding her hand and never taking his eyes from her for long.

He kissed her at her door, chastely, like he was trying to be a gentleman, then said goodnight. But later, when the nightmares came back, and she was frozen and terrified in her bed, Tagan appeared as if he'd known her fear was coming. As if he'd known she would need him.

He slid under the sheets and lay in bed beside her, then pulled her close and stroked her mussed hair until it was smooth.

And she fell asleep again, all safe and warm and his.

EIGHT

Brooke stretched her toes toward Tagan, but found his side of the bed empty and cold. Frowning, she cracked her sleepy eyes open, then sat up. The soft *tink tink* of metal on metal sounded from somewhere outside.

From the soft, gray light peeking in through the crack between the blackout curtains she'd put up, it was early in the morning. He probably had to go to work soon, but still, she was a little disappointed he hadn't said goodbye. After last night, he was vital to her now.

A louder clang of metal sounded, and she slipped from bed and turned off the humming window unit to hear better. She slid her boots over her pink flannel pajama pants and pulled her coat on to cover her northern half, because she was definitely not putting a bra on this early.

Tagan wasn't in the bathroom or the living room. Water splashed onto her face and teeth brushed, she pushed the door open to investigate the grating noise.

Tagan looked up from the side of her car where a pile of tools sat haphazardly. His hands were covered in grease, and he was holding a metal bar of some sort. He gave her a megawatt smile and said, "Your brakes won't squeak anymore. I replaced them. They were due."

"You changed my brake pads?"

"Yeah." He stood, looking worried. "Is that okay? I don't like the thought of you going down those back roads with old brakes."

"That's..." Oh God, she was not going to turn into an emotional crybaby first thing in the morning. "That's the sweetest thing anyone has ever done for me."

"That's sad," he deadpanned, and she laughed. When the tools were back in the bucket that had been overturned, he stood and wiped his hand on a rag that had been hanging out of his back pocket. He approached slowly, but she'd be damned if he'd go back to treating her like just another friend after last night. She jumped off the last porch stair and catapulted herself into his arms.

He chuckled and squeezed her tight. "You're going to get me in trouble, woman."

"How? By hugging you?" She clung to him tighter, and he lifted her until her feet came off the ground.

"Connor is gonna maim me."

"Connor can get over it."

Tagan winced and set her back on her feet. "Yeah, about that—"

"T, you ready?" Denison asked from the front of his trailer. He was loading a lunchbox into the passenger seat of an old beat-up Bronco. "Hey, Trouble." He greeted Brooke with a cheeky grin. "I shoulda known you were gonna come in here and stir things up."

"I like the name Trouble more than princess."

"What about Trailer Park Princess?" Haydan asked as he jogged down the stairs of his trailer next door.

"Veto," she called out. "Hey," she said, turning to Tagan. "Can I come to the job site with you guys today?"

"It's not safe up there, and you'll be bored. I don't think that's a good idea."

"I'll sit somewhere out of the way, and I won't bother you, I swear. I want to see what you guys do all day up in those mountains. Plus, I want to bring my sketch book and draw a new place. I was thinking of switching mediums for today and see if that'll loosen me up a little. I can't draw Markus's face forever."

"Markus," Tagan repeated darkly. "That's your attacker's name?"

"Yeah." She frowned. She hadn't said his name out loud that she could remember, and just now, she'd skated right over it without it shredding her. Huh. "I swear you won't even know I'm there."

Tagan sighed and hooked his hands on his hips, then stared at Denison's Bronco.

"I'll make us lunch," she said, bribing him.

Tagan's dark eyebrows arched, and he cocked his head at her. "You must really want to go."

She laughed and bit him gently on the shoulder. "Saucy man. Wait for me. I need twenty minutes."

"Denny," he called out. "I'm taking my truck up there. I'll come up right after you."

"Okay, bossman," Denison said with a wave. "See you up there, Trouble." He winked at her, as if he'd heard everything she'd said from way over there. Then he hopped into the driver's seat while Haydan took shotgun.

Connor got in the back seat, but his hard glare never left Tagan until the door was shut behind him.

"Get to it," he said, giving her a swat on the rump. "I'm gonna go clean up real quick and put the tools away, then I'll be over to help."

Excited, Brooke bounded up the stairs, put the bacon in the skillet for a couple of BLTs, and got dressed in record time while it sizzled away in the kitchen. By the time Tagan came through the front door, she'd figured out what he meant by not cooking bacon in a trailer kitchen. The vent was worthless, blowing the air right back in her face, and didn't suck the bacon-flavored smoke outside at all. And now the entire trailer smelled like breakfast. Her clothes would probably smell like it until she got a minute to do laundry.

"You were right," she muttered under her breath.

He boomed out a laugh and promised to cook the bacon in the fire pit next time she had a hankering. When the sandwiches, baggies of chips, a bowl of fruit salad, crackers, and cheese cubes sat in the bottom of a cooler, she shoved her sketch book and a set of charcoals in her satchel and headed for the bedroom to grab a hair band.

"Did you have breakfast already?" she called out, thinking Tagan was still in the kitchen, impatiently waiting on her.

"Yeah, but I'm still hungry." He was leaning against her bedroom door with a wicked smile on his face.

Heat crept up her neck as she tried to hold his naughty gaze. "Hungry for what?"

His gaze dropped to her thighs and he nodded his chin once. "You know what."

"Wait, you mean..." She screwed up her face. "You want to do that? To me?"

"Hell, yeah," he said, stalking her slowly.

She backed up until the backs of her knees hit the bed. Folding onto it, she sighed. "I've never—"

"Good."

She squeaked as he pulled her pants down, panties and all. It was daylight, and she'd never been comfortable enough to be naked in front of a man in full light.

"I like Denison's name for you. Trouble." He threw her pants in the corner and ran his hands down her bare thighs. "I knew you were trouble the second I saw you."

"Why do I get the distinct feeling you like trouble?"

He chuckled low and pulled her legs until she was situated at the edge of the mattress. "You are the sexiest looking trouble I've ever found."

"Yeah?" Her blush became a little cooler on her cheeks. "I think you're sexy, too. Hey, aren't you going to be late to work?"

"I'll make you come fast," he promised, apparently confident in his abilities. Cocky, sexy man.

"This doesn't sound fair for you," she muttered, staring at the ceiling and wishing she was as self-assured in her body as Tagan was with his.

"I'll take care of us both," he rumbled, his breath warm against the inside of her knees.

He pushed her legs open farther and Brooke held her breath. Why would anyone willingly—oooooh. Tagan bit the insides of her thighs gently, then kissed her from her knees to her sex, slowly. Now, her legs were spreading without his help. She'd always fantasized about what this would feel like but had never been tempted to ask someone to do this to her. Tagan seemed to be enjoying himself just fine. When she lifted her head, he was unzipping his pants to unsheathe his huge erection.

The first kiss between her legs was scary. The second was awesome. The third had her bones melting and on the fourth, he pressed his tongue into her and had her hips moving instinctively.

The sound came from his throat, the growl she'd come to love, and vibrated against her clit as he moved his tongue against her. Lapping, sucking, licking, and she was already on the verge of tipping over the edge. It was so wet, so warm, so special sharing this with Tagan. Tentatively, she ran her fingers through his hair and rocked her hips against the perfect rhythm he'd set.

Moaning, she spun out of control, helpless to stop the noises tumbling from her throat, which seemed to spur him to thrust his tongue deeper. Breathless and arching against him, her body clenched in pleasure as she came hard. Her body pulsed as Tagan pulled away and pushed her shirt up. He was stroking himself, long and slow, and she watched a single bead of moisture form at the tip of his cock. God, he looked beautiful like this, arms flexed, jaw tight, his gaze on her like she was the sexiest thing he'd ever seen. She wiggled under him more and lifted her shirt higher as his stroking became faster and harder. Propped on one arm, he leaned forward like he was right there—right on the edge.

Brooke ran her hand up his tricep with the tattoo and gripped him there as the first jet shot onto her stomach. With each that followed, she reveled in how he made her feel. Adored, as if she was beautiful in Tagan's eyes. Warmth trickled down her sides and onto the covers, but she didn't care.

She freaking *loved* this.

She loved him.

Her eyes went wide at the thought. She loved

him? She hadn't used that word since her college boyfriend. Love. *Love?* Yes. As she watched Tagan's chest heave and eyes close against the pleasure of his release, she knew it was true. She'd never felt more right than she did right now with him. And it wasn't because he was amazing at naked parties. It was the in-between moments, too. Holding her when she had nightmares, waking early to change her brake pads, making sure she had everything she could need at the barbecue last night. He was a man she could be happy with. And to make him happy in return, she needed to fix herself. Needed to heal from what her attacker did to her heart, so she could be open to Tagan's affection. So she wouldn't hurt him.

From this moment on, she was going to fight for herself, and in doing so, she was going to fight for Tagan.

He deserved a strong woman.

NINE

"So, you guys are called the Ashe Crew because you live in the Asheland Mobile Park, right?" Brooke held onto the grab handle to save herself from smashing her head against the window of Tagan's truck.

The roads were washed out and dangerous, but Tagan was sitting there with his arm draped across the wheel like the jarring didn't bother him at all.

"The Ashe Crew has been around for a very long time. That trailer park was named after us."

"But those trailers look about thirty-five years

old. You can't be a day over thirty."

"Not named after us exactly, but the others in the Ashe Crew before our time. Ashes hadn't been on this land for a decade before the sawmill opened back up."

"Then why aren't there any older men in your crew. You guys all look the same age."

The side of Tagan's lip twitched, and he looked out the side window, as if he was hiding his eyes from her. "There aren't many old-timers left. Too many rules, and when times started changing, they struggled to adjust. They battled each other into oblivion."

"Like lumberjack wars?" How had she never heard about this before?

"Sort of. Not all of us are lumberjacks. Some are firefighters, some are homesteaders or ranchers. We usually lock up with others who earn the same living. And usually that living includes physical labor. It keeps our...it keeps us centered. Keeps us calm and able to live normal lives."

"I don't understand. So, crews are like an underground club? Like a motorcycle club or something. Or a gang?"

"Sure."

His voice said he wouldn't give any more on that topic, so she made a crafty switch. "So, the Ashes, the Boarlanders, and the Gray Backs are all lumberjack crews."

"The Boarlanders are cutters. They switch back and forth between our site and the Gray Back's. They go down the mountainside and cut the trees. Look," he said, pulling to a stop and pointing.

Sure enough, the side of a hill was covered in felled trees. They looked like messy stacks of toothpicks from here. At the top was what looked like a work area with gigantic machines.

"They leave one tree up called a lift tree. They pick a big sturdy one, and that's what we attach the cables to." He dragged his finger through the air, across a long cable traveling down the mountain. "That's called the skyline. We have a machine that can haul logs up using that, but they need a crew down there attaching the cables to the lumber. That's my job."

She found it fascinating and leaned forward. Pointing to an enormous red machine with a long arm off to the side of the clearing, she asked, "What's that machine called?"

"That's the processor. Connor runs that one. Watch the arm there."

Finger-like metal appendages reached down the hill to a pile of rough logs. With one in its grip, the tree was pulled through the claws and stripped of its limbs, then the ends were cut off to make a clean log.

A trio of logs was hooked to cables hanging off the skyline, and they were dragged up the side of the mountain so fast, she gasped. "Isn't it dangerous being down there with that kind of equipment flinging all around?"

"Very. It's dangerous up on the landing, too. You have to keep your head at all times and make sure you trust your crew. And," he said, reaching into the back seat. "You always wear a hard hat. Always." He placed the cold, yellow thing over her head and made sure it was snug before he pulled on his own. "I'm going to set you up behind the landing and well out of the way of the cables so I don't spend the day worrying about you. Promise me you won't go wandering around though, okay?"

"Okay, I promise." She gave a private smile and looked at the passing trees as Tagan sped up again.

"What?" he asked.

"Nothing."

"Brooke," he growled out.

"I just think it's cute when you get all worried and protective."

"Yeah well, protective instincts are part of the territory with me now. Especially after what we did last night." The last part was mumbled, as if he didn't mean for her to hear it.

Tagan parked near Denison's Bronco and jogged around the front of the truck while she finagled the cooler out of the back. He opened her door and reached over her lap to help. Her breath froze in her throat as her body instantly responded to him, her nerve endings electrifying. He gripped her waist and snuck a glance to the landing, then back. With a naughty grin, he dipped forward and nipped her lip. "You want to wear my jacket today?" he asked in a gruff voice.

"So you can be reminded about last night? No, no, no. You need to be careful out here, remember. Since it's so dangerous and all." She kissed him again, gently, just a peck to show him she cared. "But thank you for the offer."

"You know, it wasn't just for me," he argued. "The wind is harsher up here in the hills, and your jacket is too thin." His gaze dipped to the crease between her legs. "You could put it over your lap."

She tapped on his hard hat thoughtfully with her fingernails, then nodded. "You win. I'll bring your jacket."

His grin grew bigger, reaching his eyes until they danced. "Good. I like the thought of it on your lap even better." He leaned forward and whispered into her ear, "Because then it'll smell like you, all hot and ready for me." He nibbled her earlobe, tickling her until she giggled and shoved his shoulder.

"You have a one track mind, you little beast," she said, trying to look serious. From the amusement swimming in his eyes, she'd failed.

"I am a beast," he declared. His smile faded. "You'd do best to remember that." He grabbed the cooler and helped her from the truck, then led her up the hill to a group of large boulders well out of the way of danger, but where she could see everything going on. "Lunch is in three hours," he said. "I'll come get you."

"Hey," she said as he made to leave. "I like you."

A slow, hopeful-looking smile crooked his lips. "I like you, too, Brooke." Gathering her hands in his, he kissed her knuckles lightly, like he had in the grocery store, then jogged nimbly down the hillside toward the landing.

Her hands were warm where his lips had touched her skin. His jacket smelled like him, woods and man and some sort of crisp, clean-smelling body wash, and something more in the undercurrents. She pulled another breath and frowned in concentration. Animal? The mixture of his scents was so alluring she inhaled three more times before she settled the jacket onto her lap and pulled her art supplies from her satchel.

The next few hours she spent in observation. Time flew as she tried to figure out everyone's job. Tagan seemed to be the boss up here, but he worked down with the crew. He held a walkie-talkie, and from where she sat, seemed to speak to Kellen, who ran the main machine that dragged logs, and Connor on the processor. In between hauls, he, Denison, Brighton, and Bruiser hooked giant cables around felled logs, then ran to the edges of the clearing to get out of the way of the machinery that dragged them up the hill. She couldn't even imagine how awful it would be for one of her friends to get caught under those lumber-heavy cables. It rocked with power and dragged the logs so fast it could crush the crew with one little misstep.

To eradicate those awful thoughts, she pressed charcoal sticks to sketch paper and shadowed and smudged with her fingers to sculpt the pictures she wanted. She'd meant to draw the new scenery since it was absolutely beautiful up here if she ignored the strip of felled, dead logs down the mountainside. But instead of drawing pines or birds or the river that snaked through the valley below, she drew Tagan. And not just Tagan, but the machinery and the other men as well. She tried to capture the seriousness in Kellen's eyes when he turned in the seat of the machine he worked, and the focus on Tagan's face when he was making sure his crew was out of the way and safe. She drew Denison's grin after he told a joke and Brighton as he stood on the landing with his back to her with the wide world beyond.

"Those are pretty good," Connor said from behind.

Brooke gasped and jumped so hard, her charcoal

skittered across Haydan's eyebrow. "You scared me," she said, closing the sketch book. It felt weird to share her unfinished drawings with him.

"Didn't mean to. I asked Tagan if I could show you around the landing while they hook up the next bunch of logs." His voice sounded bitter, as if it tasted bad that he had to ask Tagan for permission on anything.

She looked down the hill at Tagan, who was watching her with his hands on his hips. He nodded once. He had told Connor he could show her around then.

"Okay," Brooke said, unsteadily getting to her feet.

She gathered her things, but Connor took the satchel and shouldered it. "Let me," he said, folding Tagan's jacket over his forearm and offering her a hand as she climbed down the boulder. With a polite smile, she hid her desire for Tagan and his touch right now. After she slipped her palm from Connor's, she made her way down the hillside with him.

Drew was sawing loops of cables, and he looked up and grinned as they passed. A whistle blasted, and she hunched into herself against the noise. It had been sounding all morning, but down here, it was almost deafening.

"That's Denison letting Kellen know he is clear to drag the lumber up the hill. It means everyone is out of the way," Connor explained.

"Oh."

A whistled sounded from farther off, and she looked at him with arched eyebrows.

"That's the Gray Backs. Their site isn't too far away. Close enough for us to hear their whistle."

"Doesn't Kellen get confused between the two?"

"Not now. If our boss moves our sites closer together, it could cause a problem." His blond hair fluttered in the breeze under his hard hat, and dimples bracketed his mouth as he smiled and dragged his gaze from her boots to her eyes. "Damn girl, you do look good in a hard hat."

Brooke narrowed her eyes. "You work the processor, right?"

Lightning cracked in the distance, and the clouds above let off the first drops of an early spring storm. Cold splats of water hit her arms as she crossed them over her chest like a shield.

"Come on, I'll show you the machine I work. The

boys will stop for lunch soon, but we've got a few minutes."

The cab of the machine was small but fit them both comfortably...if she sat on Connor's knee, which he insisted on until she growled and gave in. He showed her all the levers and what they did, and then he placed her hand on the main one and guided her through picking up a log and stripping it. She had to admit, having control of heavy machinery was empowering and addictive. She did three more logs with Connor's help, then one by herself. It was then that she noticed Connor's hands on her waist, his thumbs stroking her back.

Stiffening, she jerked away from him. "I think I should go."

"Go where?" he asked, gripping her waist again.

"Stop it, Connor. I'm with Tagan." She didn't know why she said that. They weren't to the phase yet when they were claiming each other publicly, but Connor was way too handsy for her comfort. He was charming and handsome, but sometimes his eyes went cold, like they were doing now, and he reminded her of Markus.

"He has no claim to you, Brooke. That's not how

this works. Not up here with us."

"What?" she asked, backing out of the doorway.

Connor stood and ducked the frame. "Tagan has to abide by rules, just like the rest of us do. You aren't with him, Brooke. You aren't with anyone. I have just as much right to you as he does."

The metal steps had grown slick in the rain that was coming down harder now. Panic clogged her throat. Markus had followed her like this, stalked her until she was cornered. She wouldn't let that happen again with another man as long as she lived. Swallowing a whimper, she climbed down the side of the machine as fast as she could.

"What are you doing?" Connor yelled and grabbed her jacket.

A scream lodged in her throat as she bucked away from his touch, away from Connor and Markus and anyone who wanted to hurt her. Her vision blurred with her frantic need to escape, and she lurched out of her jacket. Losing her balance, she tumbled down the last step and tried to catch herself on the grate.

The scream she'd tried to swallow burst out as Connor reached for her and missed. Pain, jagged and dark, slashed up her arm as she caught sharp metal and tumbled to the ground. She landed hard in the damp dirt below. Her tailbone ached, but that wasn't what had her gasping in pain. Her hand wept red from a deep gash across her palm. Her nerve endings were burning, and she clutched it to her chest so she wouldn't see the crimson anymore.

"Fuck, why did you do that?" Connor yelled. "I was trying to catch you and you jerked away from me!" He jumped to the ground beside her, looking pissed.

His shadow covered her as tears streamed down the side of her face, but he disappeared with a grunt.

"Let me see it," Tagan said softly, suddenly there. He tugged at her hand and opened her fingers with a gentle touch. "Shit." He stood and glared at Connor, who was sitting in the mud with a look of pure hatred. "I said you could show her around, Connor. I trusted you not to let her get hurt."

"She jerked away from me when I was trying to catch her!"

"Were you pushing up on her?"

Connor's eyes narrowed. "I have just as much right to her as you do. More so even. I called her. I saw her first."

"So that's a yes. She's an abuse victim, you asshole. You can't handle her like that! She's not some plaything you claim as your own like some spoiled child."

"But the rules say—"

"Fuck the rules." Tagan was yelling now, and red crept up his neck until he looked truly scary. His eyes looked different. His face looked savage.

Brooke stood slowly, clutching her throbbing hand to her stomach. "It's okay. It was my fault. I felt cornered and panicked. Please don't fight."

All of the men gathered around them now, shifting their weight like they were uncomfortable. Kellen shoved through the crowd and pulled her hand out to examine it. Her palm felt like it had been lit on fire when he pried her fingers open.

"Fuck the rules?" Connor asked, blond eyebrows arched high. "Those rules are in place to keep us safe. To keep us alive. To keep us from killing each other like the old-timers did!"

"No, this rule is an old-timer rule. It's archaic and doesn't fit anymore."

"The claiming rule is archaic?" an unfamiliar man

asked from the outskirts of the loose circle.

The change in the Ashe Crew was instant. Lowering themselves, tilting their chins to expose their necks, casting their eyes downward. Kellen sank to his knees beside her, but Tagan remained upright, his shoulders rigid as he backed protectively in front of her.

"That's right," Tagan snarled, his voice dipping low and gravelly. "Choosing a woman shouldn't just be on the man. She should have a say in it, too."

"Choosing a woman? Don't you mean choosing a mate, Second?" The man stepped into the center of the circle. He was tall and lean as a whip. He stood straight, his chin high as he looked down at her, as if he knew his place in the world, and it was on top of the food chain. His sandy brown hair was cropped short, and he had the most unusual color of brown-green eyes.

His hand snaked out and grabbed hers in a lightning fast move. She moaned in pain as he spread her fingers wide. She struggled to rid herself of his agonizing grasp, but he held on tighter with surprising strength. "You aren't healing." He slid a cold glance to Tagan. "And she smells like you.

Fucking a human, are we?" He made a clucking sound behind his teeth and shook his head.

His words made her insides turn to jagged shards of ice. A human? Connor stood, and a slow smile transformed his face to something wicked.

"Don't." Tagan inched closer to her and cocked his head, his eyes pleading with the stranger. "Please don't, Jed. She can leave. She's not a part of this place."

"Ha," Jed huffed out. "Not yet."

He yanked her arm and threw her into the center of the circle. She landed hard in the mud on her hands and knees and whimpered at the pain in her hand as it hit wet earth.

"I got a call from Connor yesterday that brought me back early. He said a challenge has been issued." Jed rolled his head and glared at Tagan with an empty smile. "Now, you know how much I like a good bear fight."

Tagan crouched down in front of Brooke, and a snarl ripped through his body.

Brooke's heart was pounding so hard her chest hurt. She couldn't catch her breath as panic choked her. What had she stumbled into? She thought these were her friends, but maybe she was wrong.

"Jed," Kellen said. "Tagan's right on this one."

Jed reached back and slapped Kellen across the cheek. But when Brooke looked back at him, four perfect, deep claw marks were etched into his skin, and Jed's nails now looked inhumanly long.

"Holy shit," she whispered. "Tagan, what's happening?" She touched his back, but the muscles there were stiff and unyielding. His only answer was the furious-sounding, inhuman growl that rattled from his chest. This wasn't like the one he gave her when he was happy. This was the most dangerous sound she'd ever heard.

"I forbid you to change," Jed spat out at Kellen. He jabbed a finger at Denison and smiled cruelly. "I forbid you to change." He went around the circle and said it to everyone but Connor and Tagan.

The others looked at her with helpless expressions, as if they wanted to do something but couldn't. Brighton fell to his knees, gritting his teeth, and she could've sworn moisture rimmed his eyes.

"Connor," Jed said, "you issued a formal challenge for Second and for this piece of shit human. I don't know why you want her. She's not very curvy or womanly looking, and she reeks of Tagan, but hey. To each his own. You want a challenge? As your alpha, I sanction it. First to Turn her gets her."

"No!" Tagan yelled, his voice transforming to a roar that rattled the trees.

Brooke stared in horror as Connor's face elongated and his body became bigger. Fur shot from his skin, dark and thick, and with a series of pops that sounded like snapping bones, an enormous grizzly bear burst from him.

Tagan's hand was on her leg as he pushed her backward, inch by inch. "Do you choose him?" he asked in a strained voice.

Connor-the-bear lowered to all four legs and stepped forward.

She couldn't breathe. This wasn't happening. Bears didn't come out of men. They just didn't. She blinked rain from her eyes as another sob tore from her throat.

Tagan turned and repeated louder, "Do you choose him? Do you choose this life?"

"No!" she screamed. Of course she didn't fucking choose Connor. He was a bear! A bear who was stalking closer like he was going to kill her.

"Brooke," Tagan said. The seriousness of his tone pulled her attention. "Run."

"I don't understand—"

"Run!" he bellowed, his voice sounding fearsome as it tapered off into a snarl.

Chest heaving, she backed away slowly. Her body felt numb. If she tried to escape now, her legs would lock up and she'd fall again.

Tagan stood slowly in the fine mist as Connor charged, shaking the earth with every pounding step.

And just as he reached Tagan, a blond-colored grizzly exploded from the man she loved.

"Bear, bear, bear," she chanted under her breath as the two locked in a violent battle.

"Run, Brooke," Kellen gritted out. His face sagged, as if the effort to say that had leeched his energy. Red dripped in rivers down his face, but already, the slashes across his cheek were beginning to close. "Please," he begged in a broken whisper.

And suddenly, she wasn't numb anymore. She wanted to live. She'd survived Markus, and her drive to outlast Jed's sick order was enough to dump adrenaline into her veins and make her want to fight. Legs pumping, she blasted through the circle and away from the bears. An echoing slap and bellow of pain sounded, and she flinched, hoping desperately that Tagan would be okay. He was back there trying to protect her. She didn't understand any of this. Couldn't wrap her head around what had just happened, but she knew that deep down, bear or not, Tagan was trying to buy her precious time.

She ran down the slippery road, her boots growing heavier with each step as mud caked them. Pushing her legs harder, she lifted her knees higher to accommodate the added weight. The pain in her hand was nothing but a dull ache now as she ran for her life. She threw the door to Tagan's truck open and scrambled in as fast as she could.

"Key, keys, keys," she whispered, searching frantically for them with trembling fingers. Glinting metal shone from the cup holder, and she grabbed the jingling chain and jammed the biggest key into the steering column. The engine turned and roared to life.

She'd done well not to look behind her, but now, with the truck facing the landing, it was impossible for her to avoid it. She had to see if Tagan was okay before she spun out of here.

Fumbling to turn on the windshield wipers, her eyes went wide as she got a glimpse of the dark grizzly, Connor, charging her way with Tagan on his heels. With a shriek, she jammed the gas and spun out in a wide circle, the tailgate hovering right at the edge of the road before she straightened out and fishtailed her way down toward the trailer park.

She was sobbing now, trying hard to fit the world into what it used to be. One where she wasn't called a *human* like it was a curse word and where giant snarling bears didn't live inside of men.

Tagan was a bearman. A werebear? He'd played her. Strung her along as if they had a chance at a future. So many secrets. Clearly he was part of a world she didn't understand and didn't belong in, and now because she'd unknowingly gotten in too deep, she was fighting for her life. Tagan was fighting for her life, too.

She should've left Asheland Mobile Park that first day, just like her instincts had screamed for her to.

Her rearview mirror was terrifying. It showed Connor gaining on her. Tagan slammed him against the side of the mountain, but the dark-furred grizzly wouldn't be deterred. His eyes seethed with rage—a black fury that said he was going to kill her.

She was already going dangerously fast but pressed the gas to the floorboard anyway. If she flew off the side of the cliff, it would be a less painful death than the one that was coming for her. At each curve, she drew nearer to the edge of the road as she slid this way and that. Desperate to keep control of the truck, she gripped the steering wheel until her knuckles went white. The tail end of the truck flew sideways and smashed into the rock face that shot up toward the heavens. She lurched in her seat and screamed as she tried to straighten out again.

Connor hit the back of the truck again, and as soon as she gained control, a quick peek into the rearview showed Tagan lunging and sinking his teeth into the dark bear's neck. She sped off and left them there, wiping her rainwater soaked hair away from her eyes. She narrowed her gaze on the road in front of her and vowed that she was going to make it out of this alive.

The road led right past the trailer park. The truck had been damaged in Connor's attacks and made a metallic clanking noise that grew louder and louder by the moment. She hit the gravel road to the trailers but slammed on her brakes when she almost barreled into a massive gray-colored bear.

"I don't understand," she whispered. Jed told his crew they couldn't turn into bears, right? It sounded important when he'd said it, as if they couldn't disobey. So why was this bear allowed to break the rule he'd set?

Her eyes went wide as he stood to his full height in front of her.

Unless this was Jed.

"Oh, shit," she murmured.

The bear stood between her and the Volvo, and Tagan's truck sure wasn't going to make it to town with the noises it was making. She needed her car to escape. Gripping the wheel, she screamed, "Come on!" and slammed her foot onto the gas.

Jed charged, but she stayed the course until the last possible moment. Then she slammed on the brake and jerked the wheel, spinning the truck until the back of it smashed into the bear.

The driver's side door ripped off before she'd recovered from the deploying air bag.

Jed's empty, soulless eyes glared at her in

triumph as he reached a giant paw into the cab of the truck.

She slid as far away as she could, but it wasn't enough. She was going to die after all. After everything she'd been through, everything she'd lived through, her life was going to end at the claws of a monster.

A flash of gold blasted across the front window and Jed toppled backward with a furious roar.

Tagan. He was here, still fighting to add minutes to her life.

Boneless, she fell out of the opening Jed had ripped into the truck. On wobbly legs, she ran for her trailer. The keys to her Volvo were inside 1010, and she was going to lose precious seconds retrieving them, but it couldn't be helped.

The rhythmic breathing of bears dragged her frightened gaze behind her just as she reached the center of the park. She was horrified to realize Tagan and Jed were both racing toward her, Tagan in the lead. She ran faster, her legs threatening to freeze with her fear.

With a grunt, Tagan knocked her legs out from under her, and she fell forward, nose inches away from the Volvo's back tires. His eyes were sad as he leaned his big block head toward hers. They seemed to apologize for every wrong that had ever been done.

She didn't understand. Jed was coming. Why had Tagan pinned her here in the dirt? "Tagan?" she whispered, terrified.

He curled his lips back, revealing impossibly long canines. His eyes dipped to the scar Markus had left on her neck with a look of such regret.

She screamed as Tagan sank his teeth into her shoulder.

TEN

Brooke's body went rigid, as if she'd been electrified. Pain stabbed down her shoulder, eased, then shot farther, reaching into her chest. Clenching her teeth, she threw her head back and gritted out a groan. She'd never felt pain like this. Tagan had sunk his teeth into her shoulder until he hit bone, but that couldn't be what was causing her body to seize like this.

Agony spread through her with inky tendrils, growing bigger and fuller until she was filled with glass edges that shredded her insides to pieces. She cried out as she burned.

Tears streamed down the corners of her eyes as she clenched her hands against what was happening to her. Tagan watched her with the saddest look she'd ever seen in an animal's eyes.

The ground shook as Jed charged, but when Tagan stepped out of the way, the giant gray bear skidded to a stop beside her. His nostrils flared, and his eyes sparked, but he didn't add to her pain. He didn't attack. He only stood there, watching and waiting for...something.

The pain drained from her arms and legs and centered in her middle, writhing like some snake caught in her gut. Her breaths came in short pants, so fast, she thought she'd faint.

Tagan had done this to her. She was dying, and it was all his fault. "Why?" she rasped out.

Tagan shook his head slowly and stood over her. Lowering himself to his elbows, the blond bear scooped up her crumpled body and pulled her against his chest. She wished his closeness comforted her now, but she was on fire in the middle. She was burning alive.

His fur tickled her cheek, and she clutched onto

his side, grasping his hide in her clenched fist. The tears came harder as she imagined dying without ever finding out why he'd betrayed her like this.

The fire burned hotter inside of her, and she squeezed her eyes tightly closed and pressed her face against his wet fur. His heartbeat pounded against her belly.

No, not his heartbeat. That *bum, bum, bum* was coming from within her. Now it was growing stronger and faster. This was it. The pain was blinding with each pulse, and she bowed her back when she couldn't stand it anymore.

She shattered.

Grew, broke, reshaped. Red fur shot from her body like a million needles pricking her skin at once. Claws ripped open her hands, and her scream of anguish tapered to a feral-sounding bellow.

Tagan stumbled backward, and his soft blue eyes went wide as his gaze trailed across her new form. Jed curled his lips once, then meandered off toward the trees.

She wasn't dead.

Looking down at her fur, shining auburn in the clouded light, she huffed a breath. Steam curled from her long muzzle. She heaved herself upward and stood, unsteady, on all fours, legs splayed like a newborn colt. This new body was powerful. She raked her front claws through the dirt, and it tilled the earth as if they'd been made to do just that. Her breath slowed as she dragged her gaze back to Tagan.

His muzzle was darker than the longer fur that covered his back and legs. His chest rose and fell as he watched her. In size, he was enormous compared to her. From here, she could make out each fine whisker near his nose and hear every beat of his heart. Her senses were overwhelmed with the wet smells of the forest. Evergreen sap, moss, blood, animals, damp dirt...she could identify it all.

What if she was trapped as a bear forever?

Dragging a long breath of air, she scrambled backward until her stumped tail hit the park fence. *Change back, change back, change back!* Closing her eyes, she concentrated on what she used to look like. Long blond hair, champagne-colored eyes, dark lashes, lips a little on the small side... The bear who'd stolen her skin didn't go away.

The other men in Tagan's crew appeared out of the mist like apparitions. They looked as uncertain as

Tagan did.

All but Kellen. Kellen was smiling. "So we can keep her?" he asked.

The world began spinning, and the lightheadedness only got worse as she tried to take a step forward. Her breathing became shallow, and she closed her eyes against the urge to retch. Her hide went cold under her fur, and her hair stood on end, making her body tingle.

The horizon went belly up as she swayed and hit the ground.

The last thing she saw was Tagan charging toward her, just like he had before he'd turned her into a monster.

****

Brooke opened her eyes to gray morning light filtering through the edges of her blackout curtains. Her new senses told her she wasn't alone in her room, but she was hurt and not in any rush to face the man who'd turned her into what she was now.

She lifted her hand and stared at the long cut she'd gotten from the processor yesterday. Already, it was almost healed. More proof she wasn't the same— wasn't human anymore.

She clenched her hand into a fist and sighed, then rolled over to face her demons.

Tagan was sitting in a chair against the wall, elbows on his knees, hands clasped in front of his mouth, staring at her. He looked like he hadn't moved in ages. Kellen, Denison, and the others stood and sat in various positions around the room, quiet and somber as she looked at each one in turn.

"Go on," Tagan said low. "She's okay."

One by one, they came and touched her knuckles on the hand that had been hurt. None of them said a word, and none of them met her eyes. Then they left her alone with Tagan.

"I'm not okay," she said in a hoarse voice.

"I know. I didn't know what else to do."

"You could've not bit me." Her voice wrenched up an octave as fury flooded her veins.

"Jed was going to kill you. I broke the rules by fighting Connor instead of racing him to Turn you. Jed doesn't kill his own kind, though. Not anymore. Turning you was the only way I could think to save you."

"Where is Connor?"

"Dead."

"You killed him?"

He swallowed hard and looked away toward the window. In a choked voice, he said, "Yes. I couldn't kill my alpha, though. It took all I had just to fight Jed off you." His voice hitched as he dragged his tortured gaze back to her. "This isn't the life I wanted for you, Brooke. For us. I wanted you to have a choice about it."

"A choice about it? You marked me just like Markus did, but worse. You put a bear inside of me." She swallowed a sob and jerked her eyes to Tagan's feet with the admission that came from her mouth. "You should've let him kill me."

Tagan's face crumpled, and moisture that had rimmed his eyes fell down his cheeks. He looked ill as he covered his mouth and shook his head slowly. "Don't say that." His voice came out a whisper.

She couldn't watch him cry. It gutted her, knowing he was hurting, too. She sat up and forced the demand from her lips. "Tell me about what I am."

Tagan sniffed and leaned back in the chair, straightened one leg and stared at the toe of his work boot. "You're a bear shifter now. With practice, you'll be able to shift as often as you want—"

"I don't want that. How often do I *have* to shift?"

"Once a month at least." He lifted his eyes back to hers. "You're asking this because you're leaving, aren't you?"

"Yes." She gasped and tried not to cry at the way her heart felt like it was being ripped from her chest with the word. She didn't want to leave him. Didn't want to leave this place or the crew. She wasn't done healing yet. "I came here to get better, and now I'm…" She bit her lip and wished she was good with words. Good at making him understand they wouldn't work if she stayed and didn't deal with this away from here. "If I stay, I won't get better. I won't forgive you, and I want to. This place is amazing. It's suited for what I am now. But I wanted to come out here to get stronger, and I can't depend on you to lift me up with this. I need to get to know the animal inside of me without you dragging me up the mountain of issues I have. I need to do this on my own."

"I understand." He said the words, but his eyes looked just as betrayed as she felt right now. "When?"

She stared at him for moments, gathering her strength so her voice wouldn't crack. "Today."

His face fell, and he stood. Wiping his face on the

shoulder of his shirt, he strode to the door. At the frame, he turned and murmured over his shoulder, "I'm sorry." Then he left.

Curled in a ball on the bed, she cried for a long time. Cried for the humanity she'd lost, cried for the half-healed scars Markus had left on her heart, cried for the new ones Tagan had given her. She cried because she'd been so close to finding herself again here, only to be transformed into something totally different. She cried at having to start all over again. But most of all, she cried for what she and Tagan could've been.

Damn Jed and Connor. Damn them to hell for the wedge they jammed between her and the man she loved. It wasn't fair. None of this was fair.

With her eyes full and her heart broken, she dressed, packed her things, and made the bed. Then she took one last look at the bedroom she'd made into an art studio. Paintings of Markus still littered the floor. She stacked them all neatly into a corner and left them there. She'd miss 1010, this rickety old trailer, but she left the paintings because she wanted this place to remember she'd been here. She wanted to stamp her mark on this little home in the woods, like it had stamped itself into her heart.

When she dragged her luggage outside, Kellen was waiting for her. He took the suitcase from her hands and packed it into the trunk of the Volvo as the others stood by, looking as sad as she felt. Tagan wasn't anywhere to be seen. She knew, because she looked for him.

"He doesn't like goodbyes," Kellen said. "He told us not to beg you to stay." He looked toward Tagan's trailer, and when Kellen looked back at her, his dark eyes pooled with grief. Without another word, he opened the car door for her and stepped back beside the others.

She didn't know what to say. How did she say goodbye to people she cared about so deeply. She'd failed at making Tagan understand, and she would fail with them, too. She took a long, steadying breath and said her deepest wish instead. "I hope this isn't the last time I see you."

"Goodbye, Trouble," Denison said softly as she sank into the driver's seat.

As she pulled away, she watched them through the rearview mirror. Tagan came from his trailer at the last minute, fingers locked behind his head and chin tilted up as he watched her leave. The pain on his face almost doubled her over. She was leaving a piece of her heart in Asheland Mobile Park, and in return for saving her, she was taking a part of his with her.

She was the worst.

She had to do this, though. Tagan deserved a strong woman, and perhaps she could be that someday. It wouldn't happen here, though. Not now. Not with them coddling her the entire way.

As the trailer park disappeared out of sight, she swore she would forgive him someday.

But for right now, she had questions only Meredith could answer.

She had a life and a knot of loose ends to rid herself of.

ELEVEN

The last three months had been hell.

Tagan shouldered a log and tossed it up onto the trailer. He didn't usually show his strength this close to the log buyer, who was human and would be here any minute to check the lumber, but dammit, if he didn't work out some of his frustration, he wouldn't sleep tonight. Again.

He was alpha now.

Not because he chose to be responsible for the entire crew, but because if he hadn't challenged Jed after what he'd done, Tagan's bear would've shredded his humanity. He'd ordered Brooke to be hurt, an act that Tagan wasn't capable of letting go.

For the first two months after Brooke had left, he'd burned for vengeance. Connor's death wasn't enough to soothe the animal inside of him, and Jed had taunted him. Compared Tagan to himself. Said he practically *was* him, separated from his mate and destined for a slow descent into insanity.

But mated or not, Tagan would never treat his crew as shitty as that old-timer did, and his need for revenge coupled with the necessity for new leadership meant Jed had to go. Tagan had challenged the old alpha as soon as he was clear-minded enough. He'd stood up to Jed as soon as his bear had marinated in boiling fury just long enough to be unstoppable.

Jed had lost, and as he lay bloody, broken and panting in the dirt, Tagan had declared his first order as the new alpha of the Ashe crew. Jed was banished.

Tagan snarled just thinking about him, and hefted another log onto the trailer.

Kellen leaned against a tree, head canted as he watched him with the same worried expression he'd worn since the day Brooke left.

Sweat dripped down Tagan's face and into his eyes, and he rubbed it clean with the sleeve of his shirt. "What, Second?" he asked, lifting another log.

"Nothing at all," Kellen said.

"Say it and be done with it. I'm tired of you staring at me all the damned time."

"You're going to end up like Jed."

"Fuck, man." Tagan gripped his hips and glared at him. "You think that's the way to fix this? Compare me to the last asshole alpha?"

"Not like that, Tagan. Jed was broken because his mate left him to live in town, and he was splitting his time between his crew, and his life with her. Dominants can't do that. The people your bear needs to protect have to be in one place."

"That, and he was an old-timer determined to bury our crew into the ground," Tagan muttered. He couldn't believe his best friend was filling his head with the same crap Jed had tried to feed him. "And what do you want me to do about it? Brooke's gone. Not my choice."

"You could bring her back."

Tagan pulled his work gloves off and chucked them against the tail-light of the lumber truck.

"Kellen, you don't understand this. She wasn't my mate. Everything got fucked up before I could ask her."

"You mean before you could claim her."

"She has to claim me back, man." The words came out sounding strangled.

She hadn't picked him back. Not when it counted. Not when he needed her to tell him it was okay, and that she forgave him. The guilt over Turning her was black water he drowned in every day. And every night, he lay awake, staring at the ceiling of his trailer, wondering how he could've done it different.

Fucking Jed. Fucking Connor. Fucking him for not being strong enough to challenge Jed for alpha when it mattered—when he could've saved Brooke from being Turned.

"I miss her, too," Kellen said quietly. He approached and placed a white envelope on the end of a log hanging from the truck. "We all do."

Tagan watched him lumber away. Kellen had disappeared around a bend in the dirt road before he dared to look at the envelope again.

There was no name on the return address, but it was from Boulder. With trembling hands, he opened the flap. The paper was thick and elegant, and it seemed almost a shame that his dirty fingers smudged the fine linen stock inside.

You're cordially invited to view Stars of Ashe
Art Show by Renowned Artist Brooke Belle
June Third from 7 – 10

It had the address of a studio and a website at the bottom, and across the top were four thin panels with sneak peeks of different paintings. Recognition zinged through him. In the very last panel, a bear stood with his back to the viewer, painted in thick blacks and outlined in neon green chaotic strokes. It looked over its shoulder at the viewer. Tagan staggered backward at the rendered picture of himself on canvas.

The invitation fell into the dirt in front of him as he knelt down and scrubbed his hands over his face to stifle the pain in his heart. To stifle the joy at the idea that she still thought of him, and the hope that she'd sent him this invitation because she wanted to see him again. His mixed emotions crashed over him like an avalanche.

Two days. He had two days to get his shit together and get his mate back. To do whatever she needed. He'd beg her forgiveness if she'd give him the time.

Tagan inhaled a long, shaky breath and looked over at his reflection in the dusty hubcap of the truck. The three month beard would have to go, and even he could see the ingrained sadness in his eyes now, but maybe she'd understand.

He tore his gaze away from the reflection of his broken self. This could hurt him. If this was just an invitation to see her for an hour, then say goodbye forever, going to Boulder could destroy him. He'd be a worse alpha than Jed when he returned to his crew. It was a risk.

He drew his gaze to where Kellen had disappeared behind the trees. They deserved better than this.

His crew was broken without her.

He was a broken alpha without her.

Tagan owed it to his men, and to himself, to try to bring Brooke home.

****

"I'm nervous," Brooke admitted to Meredith as

her mentor pulled her toward another group looking at her painting titled *Cut*. All of the paintings were darker than she used to do, built up with blacks and dark grays until the canvases were thick with paint and chaotic brush strokes, but her starscapes had come back. Now, her wooded areas just had a few extras. This painting had the processor Connor had worked, with a full moon above and the bright stars she was known for smattered across the top half of the oversize painting.

"Why are you nervous? All of your paintings have already sold. And if it's the critics you're worried about—"

"No, it's not that. I'm worried Tagan won't come."

Meredith pulled her to a stop and hugged her tight. She smelled like perfume and animal, though the humans around them would never smell or suspect the latter. Brooke's heightened sense of smell had been an adjustment.

"I know my boy, and I know how he feels about you. He'll be here," Meredith promised.

Her words should've settled Brooke's pounding heart, but the show was halfway over, the paintings all sold, and he still wasn't here. Maybe she'd hurt him too badly and ruined any shot they ever had.

"Your eyes, dear," Meredith said as she eased back. "Deep breath. Good girl. Those eyes can't pass for human right now. You need to settle down. Here," she said, snatching a wine glass half-full of red from a passing server's tray. "Sip this." Meredith had become another type of mentor now. She coached her in blending in with the humans in the city, despite the bear that lived just under her skin.

Brooke downed it like a shot of whiskey and steadied her breathing. Already, she felt more in control. "Better?"

Meredith gave her a smile that crinkled the corners of her blue eyes—eyes the same shade as her son's. "Much. And look." She turned Brooke's shoulders slowly until she faced the door.

Tagan stood there in a suit, hands in his pockets as he watched her.

She couldn't help the slow grin that took her face or the emotion that stole her heart. Her Tagan. He'd come for her. Even after everything, he'd come.

She'd worn a strapless dress tonight, owning her scars like he'd taught her. No one was ever rude enough to ask her where they'd come from, and she felt empowered to be exposed like this.

His eyes followed the line of her neck, and a smile crooked the side of his lips when he saw the mark he'd left on her shoulder. He blinked slowly, then brought his gaze back to hers.

There he was, her beautiful Tagan. Confident, intense, strong, able.

Brooke took a step forward and nearly rolled her ankle on her high heel. With a low, feral-sounding snarl in her throat, she yanked her shoes off and bolted barefoot toward him.

He jogged toward her and caught her in a back-cracking hug, as if he never wanted to let go. God, she'd lived and breathed for this moment. "I put in the work," she whispered, as a warm tear slipped down her cheek. "I wanted to make you proud, so I put in the work."

"You always made me proud, Brooke."

"I Change." She eased back and cupped his face— the face that visited her dreams—the face she adored. "I Change a couple of times a week at least. Out in the woods beyond the city. Your mom taught me how."

Tagan looked at her with such wonder in his eyes. Jerking his gaze to the crowd, who were now clapping quietly, he ducked his head in a greeting to Meredith and set Brooke on her feet. Tugging her hand, he searched the paintings in the alcoves along the wall, then pulled her toward a painting she'd done called *Him and Me*. It was the one Meredith had put on the last panel on the invitations. In it, Tagan's bear had his back to hers in the moonlight, but he was looking at her over his shoulder. It was of both of them in their animal forms, up on the landing amongst the felled trees. Out of all the paintings she'd done, the stars were brightest in this one.

Pulling her close, he whispered against her ear, "Tell me more."

"The nightmares are gone. I only dream of you."

"Bad dreams?" His eyes were worried as he brushed his thumb across her cheek.

"I don't dream of when you Turned me. I never did. I guess it wasn't as scary as what Markus did to me. I dream of your face. Of you sitting in the corner of my room, watching me. And you look so sad, and it makes my heart break with how much I've missed you. But I wanted to be strong for you, Tagan. I needed time to fix the ugly places inside of me."

Her favorite rumbling noise emanated from his

chest, and she settled it with her hand.

"You were always strong to me, you beautiful, complicated, sweet woman." He leaned down and pecked her lips. "If I pay double for this painting, would you deliver it to my house in person?" he asked, his eyes serious.

"Oh." She frowned at the painting. "Someone already bought this one. It was the first one that sold before the show even began."

A slow smile spread across his lips, and he kissed her again, longer this time. He brushed his tongue against the closed seam of her lips, and she opened for him, tasting him.

"You bought it, didn't you?" she asked as he pulled away.

He nodded once. "So will you deliver it in person?"

"Tagan," she said, clenching the sleeves of his suit in her fists. God she loved him. "I was already coming home."

A warm chuckle filled his throat as he rested his forehead against hers. "Home," he repeated.

Relief nearly hummed from his body as he nipped her neck. "Trailer Park Princess is coming home. The boys will lose their shit when they see you. We've had a hard time with you away."

"What about Jed?" she asked, her lingering fear tainting the moment.

The smile faded from his lips. "Jed is banished. I'm alpha now. No one will ever hurt you again."

A server walked by and offered them wine.

"We should toast," she suggested, pulling two glasses and giving him one. She looked around at the guests in their tuxedos and formal dresses and lowered her voice. "It's boxed wine."

Tagan let out a surprised, booming laugh. "That's my girl. What are we toasting to?"

"I asked your mother lots of questions about what we are and our traditions. Someday, I'm going to make you my mate."

Tagan's eyes went wide. "Wait, what?"

"I'm going to work really hard at being the partner you deserve, and then someday, you're going to ask me to be your mate," she said matter-of-factly with a nod of her chin.

An uncertain smile crooked his lips, then disappeared. "Does that mean you forgive me?"

"No." His face fell, but she lifted his chin until he

looked into her eyes. "It means I never had anything to forgive. You saved me. I don't need to forgive you, Tagan. I need to thank you."

"Thank me?" He looked utterly baffled now.

"You helped me heal my muse. All of this," she said, gesturing at the room of people, dressed up and standing in groups, talking in front of her paintings. "All of this started with you and your Ashe Crew. My crew now, too. And then you went one step further and saved me at risk to your own life. You killed one of your own who was trying to hurt me. You went head to head with your alpha, and I understand now how hard that is for a Second to do. You banished him, Tagan, for me. And then you gave me the greatest gift of all." She placed her hand on her chest. "You gave me her—my bear."

He touched her cheek softly, just under her eye, which she knew was blazing blue with how emotional she was. She didn't have much control over her shifting eyes. Not yet.

"I can see her," he whispered.

"She might be the strongest part about me now. I didn't think so when I first Turned, but she's tough. My bear makes me braver. I don't fear people anymore. I don't get scared and have panic attacks in stairwells anymore because I know I can defend myself now."

"Yes, I imagine you can."

"I love you, Tagan. I want to come home."

He lifted his chin and looked at her with such fierce adoration in his eyes. "When?" he asked, just like he had those months ago when she'd left him.

Her happiness was so potent she couldn't contain her grin if she tried. "Today."

LUMBERJACK WEREBEAR

Want More of the Saw Bears?

The Complete Series is Available Now

Other books in this series:

Woodcutter Werebear
(Saw Bears, Book 2)

Timberman Werebear
(Saw Bears, Book 3)

Sawman Werebear
(Saw Bears, Book 4)

Axman Werebear
(Saw Bears, Book 5)

Woodsman Werebear
(Saw Bears, Book 6)

Lumberman Werebear
(Saw Bears, Book 7)

Sneak Peek

Woodcutter Werebear
(Saw Bears, Book 2)

Chapter One

Kellen Brown stared at the flower arrangements in the cooler in the produce section of the grocery store. He'd been standing here for five minutes, trying to figure out which bouquet Brooke would like best. A grin took his face. She was coming home, and everything was going to be okay again. The Ashe crew had been broken without her, but now she would be back, and they would all take good care of her so she'd never have to leave again.

His uncle used to bring his mother roses. Mom always said they were her favorite. With a frown to ward off the memories, he picked a bouquet of pink roses, then rolled the wonky-wheeled cart toward a bored-looking cashier.

"Looks like you're having a party," the woman in front of him said so softly. Even with his oversensitive hearing, he almost missed it. She was a mousey-looking woman who'd managed to hide herself completely in an oversize, red-and-black flannel shirt with clunky boots over black leggings. Her dark hair was down and long, covering most of her face.

A flash of stunning green froze him in place as she glanced at him, then away.

"Yeah," he murmured. "Brooke is coming back home. Such an occasion deserves a celebration."

The woman swiped her credit card for the small amount of groceries she was purchasing and gave him a confused look. "Well, this Brooke sounds like a lucky woman."

"She is. We all are."

The woman couldn't hold his stare—not even for a moment. He drew air into his nostrils, scenting her to see if his suspicions were true.

Fruit body wash, the soft smell that girls possess, and an undercurrent of animal struck him. "I know what you are."

"What?" the woman whispered. She gave him another flash of those stunning eyes she was trying to keep hidden, but this time, they looked scared.

"I don't know which exact animal you are, but I

know *what* you are," he clarified.

"Thank you," she said to the baffled-looking cashier who handed her a receipt. With a frown for Kellen, she practically ran out of the store, her plastic bags of food bumping her legs.

Kellen sighed as he watched her leave. He'd never been good with women, or with anyone, really. He made people uncomfortable for some reason. Tagan, his alpha, said people just didn't understand him or the way he was raised, but sometimes it felt like more than that. Sometimes it felt like he'd never be able to hold a conversation with anyone outside of the Ashe crew.

That revelation made him lonely.

There was an old Coke machine outside the store—one that sold glass bottles of soda. He always got one when he came into town, but when he saw the woman waiting on a bench out front, he bought two.

Kellen settled the cart against the backrest so it wouldn't roll away, then sat down beside her. "I'm sorry I made you mad. Forgive me?" He handed her the cold bottle and popped the top of his own.

She took the bottle slowly, leaning away from

him as if he was handing her the working parts of a bomb. "There's nothing to forgive. I don't know you."

Damn, she was good at hiding her face. He wanted to see her eyes again, but she'd pulled all that dark hair in front of her and wouldn't tilt her head his way.

"You shouldn't sit by me. My boyfriend will be here any minute to pick me up, and he'll be very angry if he sees you talking to me."

"Why?" Kellen asked.

"Why what?"

"Why would he be mad at you talking to another person?"

"Because that's the way men are. They're jealous and possessive."

"No. That's not the way they have to be. It's only the way some men *choose* to be. Here, let me." Kellen opened her soda, then handed her the metal top.

"You said you know what I am," she whispered. "How did you know?"

He smiled at a mother bustling her trio of young children across the street. "Because we're not so different." Without any thought, he reached out and ran the knuckle of his finger from underneath her chin to the base of her throat.

The woman froze but allowed it. "You shouldn't do that. My boyfriend…" She couldn't seem to find any more words.

"I'm Kellen Cade Brown," he said. When she didn't answer, he asked, "What's your name?"

Her attention darted this way and that, everywhere but at him. "I shouldn't—Skyler. My name is Skyler."

"Beautiful name for a beautiful woman," he said matter-of-factly. With a nod of his head, he tinked his bottle of soda against hers.

"Your girlfriend wouldn't like you saying those things to another woman," Skyler said.

"My girlfriend?"

"Brooke. The one you bought the flowers for."

"Oh, she wouldn't mind. She's nice."

"You're strange," Skyler muttered.

Those two words gutted him. Sure, they were true, but he hadn't wanted to hear that from her. He wanted Skyler to see him differently than everyone else did. He hunched inward against the pain. "Yeah." He choked on the word as he stood. He smiled at her but she wouldn't see it. She was still doing a bang-up job of avoiding his eyes.

"It was nice to meet you, Skyler."

Another flash of green as she canted her head, a sharp gesture that would've told him what she was, even if his nose wasn't working today. She lowered her gaze to the toes of his work boots, and he wondered if all of her kind were so submissive.

"I shouldn't have said that," she murmured. "It was mean. I'm strange, too."

"No," he said as he pulled a pink rose from the bouquet that rested in the cart and set it on the bench beside her. "You're perfect." Kellen gripped the cart handle and avoided the urge to look back at her again for the chance to see those stunning eyes once more. Pushing the cart toward the crosswalk, he gritted his teeth against the hurt in his chest.

"Kellen?" Skyler asked.

When he turned, she was standing by the bench with her face angled toward the ground holding the flower and the full bottle of Coke in front of her thighs. "I don't think my boyfriend is coming for me. Can you give me a ride to my house?"

Kellen looked around the parking lot, astounded that her asshole boyfriend would leave her here without a ride. "Sure. My truck is over there." He dragged the cart back to her, picked up her grocery bags from beside the bench, loaded them with his, and jerked his head toward his ride. "Come on."

She followed a few paces behind, and the first tendrils of suspicion curled around his heart. He couldn't tell if she was naturally submissive or if she was scared, but the idea of the latter ignited something ugly in his gut. He didn't like when women were scared.

"Are you afraid of me?" he asked when he was settled behind the wheel and she was sitting as far across the bench seat of his truck as possible.

"No, but I should be."

"No, you shouldn't. I'd never hurt you. What are you afraid of?"

"Being seen with you." Her answer was simple and honest, but it didn't do anything to stifle the flame in his stomach.

"Where do you live?"

"Take a right on West Bridge Ave and take it all the way through town. Roger owns a cabin outside of the city limits. Roger is my boyfriend," she explained.

The way she kept saying *boyfriend* bothered him.

Not because he was jealous, but because the word lacked emotion. She could've been saying *acquaintance* for as much feeling as she put in the title.

"Is Roger your mate?" he asked, testing her.

She jerked her gaze to his, then away. "You shouldn't talk like that," she warned him in a low voice.

"Is he?"

"Yes." Her voice cracked, as if she hadn't used it in a while, and the flame in his gut became brighter.

"You aren't submissive naturally, are you?"

Skyler turned the knob on the radio volume until it blared a country song at an uncomfortable level.

Fine. She didn't want to talk, and her life wasn't his business, anyhow. That's what Tagan would tell him, and Tagan knew about people. He was good at talking to them and making them feel comfortable. He was good at negotiations with the log buyers when the Ashe crew had acquired enough clean lumber to sell to the sawmill in Saratoga. If Tagan was sitting in the truck with him right now, he'd tell Kellen to drop the woman off and hightail it back to Asheland Mobile Park where home was.

A fifteen minute drive with blaring music and Skyler's occasional direction brought him to a stop in front of a large log cabin off a dirt road.

Skyler let off a shaky breath after she scanned the front yard. "Good, he's not here. Thank you for the ride." Skyler turned and graced him with a tremulous smile. "And for the flower and the Coke, too."

She was beautiful. Pert nose and high cheekbones. Thin lips in a pretty shade of pink, and those eyes. They looked even brighter surrounded by all that purple bruising.

She pushed the door open, but Kellen leaned over her lap and pulled it closed so hard the truck rocked.

"Who. The fuck. Did that to your face?"

Skyler froze, looking terrified, but he didn't give a shit if his bear was making his face look savage right now. He wanted to kill whoever dared to lift a hand to this woman—to any woman.

"He didn't mean to—"

"Bullshit. He did, and you know it. How many times?"

"Kellen—"

"How many times?" he asked, his voice tapering

to a snarl on the last word.

"Holy crap," she said, cowering against the window. "What are you?"

"Skyler, I swear to everything that is wrong in this world, if you don't tell me who did this to you, I'm not going to be able to control my shift. Who?"

"Roger."

"Your boyfriend?"

"Not my boyfriend," she admitted. "My new mate."

"Did you pick him?"

"Kellen, I don't think—"

"Tell me how it works for your kind!" He gripped the wheel until his knuckles popped and raged white.

She stared at his hands with wide eyes. "Females don't pick. Males do."

"That's all I needed to know. Buckle up."

"What? No, I have to go inside before he comes home."

Kellen shot her a warning look.

"Look, he didn't hit me! I popped off, and he pushed me. I turned to escape him and tripped on the damned mat under the sink. I fell against the corner of the countertop. This was the first time he ever got really physical with—"

"It won't be the last."

"You don't even know him!"

He huffed a humorless laugh. If this woman understood how well he knew Roger, without even meeting him, she'd stop talking and come with him. Kellen had been raised by a sonofabitch just like her mate, and he'd be hanged by the neck before he saw her end up like his mom did. "I know him well enough. Buckle up, or I'll do it for you."

"Kellen—"

With a snarl, he reached over her lap and jerked the seatbelt into place. When she was fastened in, he peeled out of the yard, shooting gravel behind them, and blasted back down the dirt road. "You plan on leaving him?"

"It's not that simple."

"It is."

"No, it's not. We obviously don't have the same traditions that you and your people do."

"Yeah? It's customary to shove on women in your crew, is it?"

"Sometimes it's just the way it has to be." Her voice rang with hopelessness.

"Horseshit. There's no excuse, no reason. You're coming home with me."

"Why?" Her voice catapulted up an octave.

"Because," he said, daring a glance at her, "I'm going to show you how a woman should be treated."

She turned her face slowly to the front window. "I'm being kidnapped."

Kellen snorted. "No, Beautiful. You're being rehabilitated."

Woodsman Werebear
Available Now

About the Author

T.S. Joyce is devoted to bringing hot shifter romances to readers. Hungry alpha males are her calling card, and the wilder the men, the more she'll make them pour their hearts out. She werebear swears there'll be no swooning heroines in her books. It takes tough-as-nails women to handle her shifters.

Experienced at handling an alpha male of her own, she lives in a tiny town, outside of a tiny city, and devotes her life to writing big stories. Foodie, wolf whisperer, ninja, thief of tiny bottles of awesome smelling hotel shampoo, nap connoisseur, movie fanatic, and zombie slayer, and most of this bio is true.

Bear Shifters? Check

Smoldering Alpha Hotness? Double Check

Sexy Scenes? Fasten up your girdles, ladies and gents, it's gonna to be a wild ride.

For more information on T. S. Joyce's work,
visit her website at
www.tsjoyce.com

Printed in Great Britain
by Amazon